I0593845

SUBTERRANEAN

Sarah Colombo

SUBTERRANEAN

SARAH COLOMBO

SPACEBOY BOOKS

Denver, Colorado

Published in the United States by:
Spaceboy Books LLC
1627 Vine Street
Denver, CO 80206
www.readspaceboy.com

First printed August 2018

ISBN: 978-0-9997862-3-9

For Jonathan

ONE

He watched her dancing, lit up like a Christmas tree. She swayed to the music–which RIFF23 identified as *All I Want for Christmas is You*, Mariah Carey (1994)–whispered in the ear of a friend, and occasionally belted out lyrics, head thrown back.

They were crammed in Georgie's living room, music spouting from a gyrating Robots are Dancing (RAD) model. She was wearing something blue on her eyelashes. They stuck together in electric clumps, blue sweat trickling down her cheeks. The rest of her face looked naked—pink and perspiring. Her sweater—the same blue as her eyelashes–featured a large, fuzzy Christmas tree draped in LED bulbs that blinked on and off.

It was an accident, noticing her. He was sipping a mulled cider while RIFF23 played his entertainment package, a collection of fifteen-second videos intended to "Keep FUN Alive." That was the motto of Fresh Unbelievable Newness, his subscription service. Sure, he was aware of the conspiracies that FUN and their ilk actually had the goal of distraction and commodification, but the theory was provided through a twelve-second clip and he didn't really have time to digest it. Someone bumped into him. The tiny drink straw in his cider was halfway to his mouth and hit his lip. Cider sloshed onto RIFF23's Screen. Ronnie looked around to figure out who bumped into him. As his eyes moved across the room, he caught sight of her.

It was as if she created a bubble that kept her and her friend aware, away from their Screens. They looked at each other. They looked around the room. The friend sometimes pulled her Screen out, thumbed through it, stuck it back in her pocket, but Blue Eyelashes never reached for hers.

Outside of the girl and her friend and the RAD, the party went like so: the man who bumped into Ronnie bumped into some more people. A group of four clustered in a corner and danced around a different RAD, playing a remix of *All I Want for Christmas is You*. They paused intermittently to snap photos, look at the photos they took, and giggle. A man sat in a corner and played a video game. A woman sat in another corner and played a video game. Gyrating oddly to a song that was neither the original *All I Want for Christmas is You* nor its remix, a hologram entertained a group in the hallway.

Blue Eyelashes let out a shriek of delight as the music changed to another song that she apparently liked. She threw her head back and started to sing along.

"Who is she?" Ronnie asked.

RIFF23's Screen showed a paused frame from the entertainment package: a dog walking on its hind legs wearing a top hat, flickering. "I don't know who she is," he said, changing his Screen to a white question mark with a black background.

"I know you don't know," Ronnie said, sipping daintily on his straw, "but find out real quick, please."

RIFF23's question mark started bouncing around. "I can't find out!" RIFF23's voice registered alarm–his voice settings automatically switching one octave higher.

"Typical," Ronnie muttered.

"And what, exactly, is that supposed to mean?" The octave rose once more.

"Forget it," Ronnie shrugged. "I need another drink." He looked around for a Robots are Serving (RAS) model.

RIFF23's Screen changed to play a loop of an erupting volcano.

"RIFF23! Calm down!" Ronnie said through gritted teeth, noticing Blue Eyelashes no longer dancing, staring at them with her mouth barely less than agape.

RIFF23 rolled out of the room.

Ronnie grabbed an eggnog from a passing RAS and drank it in one gulp. He stood holding an empty glass in each hand. Blue Eyelashes walked over to him.

The RAD spun around playing *Jingle Bell Rock.* Ronnie wasn't sure who sang it, and instinctively looked to his right for RIFF23. Her friend danced around drunkenly beside the RAD. Ronnie felt like the room grew quieter, the lights dimmed, all the faces looked up from their glowing distractions and watched as this human packaged like a present came towards him. In reality, nothing changed. No one noticed. The woman playing a video game in the corner yelled, "Yes!"

"What's all this ruckus about?" Blue Eyelashes asked. Blue sweat was smeared beneath her eyes. She wore elf shoes with curled up toes topped with bells. She shifted her weight back and forth.

"Oh," Ronnie shrugged casually, the two empty glasses bobbing up and down. She took the glasses and set them on a table behind him. "Just a little disagreement with my companion."

"I saw. He's a Robot is Friend Forever, right?" She smelled like sweat and cinnamon. There was glitter sprinkled in her hair and he stared down at the top of her head, at the silver against her pink scalp. "What were you disagreeing about?"

"Well," he started. Her left foot made a tinkling sound as she lifted it to scratch the back of her right calf. "I just asked him a question and he didn't know the answer."

She dropped her jaw in mock surprise. He wanted to wipe away the blue where it clung to the tiny lines under her eyes. He stuck his hands in his pockets. "A robot that can't answer a question? Say it ain't so!"

He guessed she was making fun of him. He shrugged.

"What was the question?" she asked. "I'm not a robot or anything but I'll see what I can do for you."

He shook his head. Smiled. Rolled his eyes. Rubbed his hand across his face. "Oh god," he choked out.

"Wow. It must have been something very serious."

"No. No. Oh god!" He ran out of the room.

It was Christmas Eve Eve Eve, Georgie's annual excuse to throw a huge party and force everyone to listen to slurred lectures about the origins of the Christmas tree in paganism. When they were younger the party was a big event, but now the old group dwindled as people got married and reproduced. Georgie started replenishing the guest list with younger and younger coworkers. Ronnie still came. Every year he got a little drunker, always on mulled cider and eggnog. Every year his despair increased as he tried to talk to people born in a different decade. Every year he drank too much and threw up around midnight.

The room he ran into for the purposes of puking happened to be Georgie's bedroom.

"Georgie, thank god!" Ronnie yelled, wiping away puke from his lips.

Georgie sat on his bed surrounded by three twenty-somethings. He wore a red, silk bathrobe. Scanning back through his blurry Christmas Eve Eve Eve memories, Ronnie realized that Georgie always wore a red bathrobe to his party. He made a mental note to make fun of him when they were both sober, preferably when Georgie was still hungover. The twenty-somethings looked at Ronnie, rolled their eyes as one, and left the room.

RIFF23 rolled in, deploying his mop. He began cleaning up the puke playing a classic, text-based frowny face: a colon and parentheses.

"Aww, thanks bud," Ronnie said. "I thought you were mad at me."

"I am mad at you, but I am also a robot with programming that makes me inclined to clean up messes."

"Fair enough."

"What the fuck, Ronnie?" Georgie called from the bed, in a voice that indicated he didn't care for a response.

"Georgie! I need your help!"

The words were the type Georgie liked to hear. He leaned back further into his bed, put his hands behind his head, and crossed his ankles. "Well," he sighed. "What is it?"

"A girl," Ronnie said. He moved to lie next to Georgie, one foot on the floor to keep the room from spinning.

"Isn't it always?" Georgie asked, scooting away from him while maintaining his laid-back posture.

"She's right out there, just dancing around to some Mary Carey."

"It's Mariah Carey," RIFF23 corrected.

"She's dancing to Maria Carey and I had my chance but I had to throw up."

"Mariah," RIFF23 insisted.

"You know, you don't have to throw up every year," Georgie pointed out. "Although I do love traditions."

"She has blue eyelashes, you know," Ronnie told Georgie as though they were already deep into a conversation about this individual, and he was in the middle of casually mentioning some of her attributes.

"Oh no..." Georgie said. He sat up.

"RIFF23 couldn't even tell me who she was," Ronnie lolled his head over on the bed to look at Georgie and give a lazy shrug. "I mean, I'm not mad at him, I love the guy, but really what's the point of having a companion, you know, if they can't help you in your time of need?"

"You're really going to need to de-program my feelings if you're going to keep talking about me like this," RIFF23 said. He wrung out the mop over his bucket, and then strategically flicked it so that some nutmeg-infused vomit water landed on Ronnie's cheek. Ronnie sniffed, coughed, leaned over, and puked again.

"I'm sorry," he said as he hocked up the last of it. "I'm really sorry, RIFF23." He reached out one arm to try to touch the bot, but RIFF23 evaded him while mopping up the new patch of vomit, his Screen returned to the erupting volcano.

"You would be into Hil," Georgie said.

"Who's Hil?"

"The one with the blue eyelashes."

"Hil," Ronnie said wistfully. "Hil! What a beautiful name."

"Not really," RIFF23 said.

Ronnie was familiar with the term "mirthless laugh," but this was first time hearing one. Georgie let out a laugh-like sound, with the sole purpose of letting Ronnie know that Georgie was wise and Ronnie was an idiot. Ronnie considered that maybe the real reason no one came to these parties anymore was because Georgie was a pretentious jerk who wore a bathrobe, but he decided he better not mention it.

"Just go into it," Ronnie sighed. He closed his eyes.

"Into what?"

"There's a whole thing you want to say, so just start."

Bill and Laura Mills gave birth to Hilary Francesca Mills approximately thirty years prior to the Christmas Eve Eve Eve party during which Ronnie puked twice in Georgie's bedroom. Hil's birth capped off a great few years in the Mills family, which started with Bill's invention of the Selfie Mirror, an unnecessary piece of personal Tech that took off in Asian markets and among Internet celebrities in the States. The mirror had been a side project of Bill's who worked for the government doing some sort of technological stuff that no one really understood. Rumor had it that right before Hil was born, he was contracted out for a top-secret government project.

No one knew exactly when Hil was born, because there was no birth announcement, which was odd. Everyone knew the due date down to the minute. Laura posted a countdown on her Profile and constantly reminded everyone about the various fruits to which the baby could be compared as she grew. The due date came and went. The ninth month passed. The Mills started to disappear from the virtual world. First their Profiles were gone, then their photos, followed by videos, interviews, and sound bites.

Some brave person had the bright idea to knock on the Mills' door. There they were: a family of three. The story has been erased up to 2,003 times, but the version handed down orally is that Bill and Laura were playing chess while Hil slept in a bassinet. The person walked right into their house. There was no door cam or companion, no alarm, no tinkling sound welcoming them.

"We wondered if anyone would come," Laura said, or maybe it was Bill, and they invited this person to have some tea and they told him some things. They told him that they were Off the Grid. Bill quit his job, which was fine since the Selfie Mirror was more than lucrative. They didn't want any photos of Hil posted anywhere. They didn't want anyone to know her birthday or what color her hair was, though she didn't have any yet. Her eyes were blue but babies sometimes grew out of that. The point was they were going to play chess or whatever and they weren't going to be anywhere online.

Hil grew up and they didn't want her to be isolated so she went to normal school and was around kids with Screens and all of that, but they were taught early on not to photograph her and not to post anything about her. When she reached adulthood, Hil continued to practice her parents' beliefs, never getting a Screen or creating a profile.

"And that's why I couldn't figure out who she was!" RIFF23 said, his Screen changing to a smiling Santa Claus giving a thumbs up.

"Yep," Georgie said. "She's unscannable."

"Unscannable," Ronnie sighed. "Well, I think I'm done puking now. I'll try again." He got up from the bed and walked toward the door.

RIFF23 made an awful coughing noise that crackled through his speakers.

"I'm really sorry, RIFF23. You know how I get at these parties," Ronnie said. He touched his hand to the smiling Santa, which changed to a displeased face: a colon with a forward slash.

"We don't have to come here," RIFF23 attempted to whisper, the sound hissing, louder than his normal voice. "There are better Christmas parties out there."

"Could both of you please get the fuck out of my bedroom?" Georgie called.

#

The party had dwindled. One RAD was spinning around by herself, playing robot music, which RIFF23 explained to Ronnie was technically better than human music, although to Ronnie it sounded like a random combination of beeps. A couple sat on a couch staring slack-jawed at a Screen. Beside them, another couple made out with no regard for the others in the room. The male videogame player was still in his corner, cussing under his breath. The hologram sat on the carpet looking around. The group that had taken all the selfies stared down at their Screens, presumably sorting through and posting their photos.

Hil was not there.

"Locate her!" Ronnie yelled at RIFF23, unnecessarily since he was right beside him.

"I can't," RIFF23 pointed out.

"Damnit," Ronnie said. "You know what this means..."

"We have to talk to Georgie again," RIFF23 changed his Screen back to the frowny face.

Her voice erupted in Ronnie's kitchen. It was a sudden, startling sound, which just as suddenly became not so startling, like it belonged there: as at home as his worn out chairs and dirty refrigerator. "Are you sitting up very straight, wearing a nice outfit?" she asked.

He called her through something named Vintage Voices, an app that connected to landline telephones. Her phone number was 2. "She's definitely rich, man. She could probably be 1 if she wanted," Georgie had pointed out.

Ronnie could feel her lips, the weight of her tongue, the exact angle of her smile in the words.

"I'm naked, in downward facing dog," he replied. He was freshly showered, his best t-shirt soft against his skin. He'd even polished his boots. His hair was combed, his eyebrows freshly tweezed.

"Uh-huh," she said. "This isn't my first rodeo, you know. You On the Grid people can't get used to the fact that I can't see you. You get ready like you're going on a date."

"What's a rodeo?" he asked. "Besides, you're assuming I want to date you, but I was just calling you up for a casual chat."

"A casual chat where you're naked with your ass in the air?"

"Very casual."

She laughed. It was the laugh of someone un-ironic, comfortable in showing open delight.

"What are you wearing?" he asked. "I mean, not like 'what are you wearing?' but just because I can't see you... never mind."

"I'm wearing a t-shirt that says 'whatever.'"

"How very cool of you."

"Yes, well, I had to choose between it and a t-shirt that said 'cool,' but I decided to go with subtle."

"Where'd you go last night?"

She sighed. His kitchen vibrated with the sound of it. "I ran into an old friend. It was a whole... it's really not that interesting..."

"Just leaving it up to fate if you'd ever see me again."

"No fate needed. I knew you would call me."

TWO

"Everything's going to be fine," Hil said, her face a specter floating in front of him. They were tucked into the dark Zen Tent, no light save the flicker of her crystal candle. Ronnie studied the way shadow intersected her face, adhering to the ridge of her nose, the centerline of her lips.

Hil began designing the ZT at the age of four. The first incarnation was called The Fort and was made out of pillows and blankets. The purpose of The Fort was to force her friends to stop playing with their Screens. "No Screens allowed in The Fort!" she would yell, and they would look up, startled, then dutifully file inside, leaving their Screens behind.

"She's so creative!" The other parents gushed nervously to the Mills. "Imagine a four-year-old building such a thing!"

The Mills looked at the pile of linens and shrugged.

The final incarnation of the ZT was an A-frame structure made of white linen and oak, filled with cushions and hand-embroidered pillows featuring phrases like 'Just Relax-zen." Hil agreed to let her friend Chele post a photo of the ZT in a life style blast, as long as her identity wasn't revealed. The blast was one of the most popular of the year, shared over 50 million times. It promoted the Disconnect movement, which encouraged followers to do one disconnected thing for fifteen minutes a day. Sleeping didn't count.

"You don't know anything," Ronnie said. It was warm and safe inside the ZT. He leaned against a pillow that said "Buddha Buddha Buddha Buddha Rockin' Everywhere." He wished the world ended at the ZT's flaps; that the enclosed space and their two bodies were all that existed.

Hil retreated from the candle so that he could just see the shape of her.

"I don't have a job anymore, Hil," he sighed.

"You'll get a new one." The words absorbed into the plush interior.

"Statistically impossible."

He felt agitated and could sense in her obscured movements that she did too. It would be better to get along, to be kind and likeable and receptive to comfort. Best of all would be to believe her. To say, "You know what? You're right." It was a type of agreeableness that Ronnie did not have in him. Often he watched himself, as if glitched and doubled, standing partially inside his body, partially out, and he whispered: "Don't say that," or "smile," or "just say 'thank you,'" but he couldn't accept the wisdom of this other self. Instead he poked and prodded and argued, rolled his eyes and let out long sighs.

#

Prior to 17:00 that afternoon, Ronnie was a children's librarian. He was one of 16 remaining in the country. It was not the type of rarity that bred celebrity, but more the type that resulted from a slow and painful process of extinction. Robots are Researching (RAR) and Robots are Managing (RAM) models replaced their human counterparts years ago, but the children's librarian was more difficult to eradicate.

The Library piloted a storytime run by a Robots are Fun Forever (RAFF) model, but it was a failure. It turned out kids under five preferred to hear stories read by a human and songs in a human voice. RAFF930 could juggle scarves better than Ronnie, but that was about it. Ronnie almost felt sorry for her, standing up there with a needy grin on her Screen, saying, "Children, are we having fun yet?" Little Tom called out, "No!"

The parents also objected to RAFF930. Being the sort of parents that still took children to storytime, they were a bit of what Ronnie's boss, RAM6166, called "hippie dippie." They enrolled their children in Nature Education, constructed mini Zen Tents, and liked the idea of a human being reading stories and singing to their children. These "dirty hippies"–which is what RAM6166 called them when she was feeling less diplomatic–were the only thing standing between Ronnie and unemployment.

It was a tenuous protection. Responding to a resurgence of early 1990s fandom, The Library decided to add a Music Video wing with Compact Disc listening stations. Conveniently, there was just enough space for this in the children's area.

The Robots On Message (ROM) model released a pressblast stating that children's services would cease. A few of the parents showed up to protest, but most just hugged Ronnie goodbye with a sad shrug and messaged him cute little drawings from their children. A few of the RARs baked him a cake, but RAM6166 missed the goodbye party due to "A maintenance appointment I really can't get out of."

#

"Well maybe you won't find the exact same job, but you'll find a different one," Hil said. He couldn't see her at all, but from the way her voice floated toward him, he pictured her lying on her back, staring at the beam of the ZT through the haze of candlelight. Her hands, bony, beginning to show age, with tidy nails she obsessively filed, were probably resting on her belly.

"I know you're trying to help," he said. He said it like more words would follow, but they didn't.

A strange sound came from her throat, almost like a growl. "Just say it."

They were nearing their one-year anniversary. The anniversary of the day he sat in his kitchen and her voice floated around him.

"I don't want to fight," he said.

"Neither do I." She sat closer to the candle now, her throat glowing with its orange tint.

"You just don't always have the tightest grip on reality."

She blinked at him. Their breath filled the ZT. She swallowed loudly. "How could I, of all people, not have a grip on reality?"

"I'm not talking about reality versus virtual reality. I'm talking about realistic thinking."

"And how is it that I don't have realistic thinking?"

He paused. "Well... because you're rich."

"Yeah. Ok," she said. She turned her head away from him.

"I don't want to have a fight," he said again.

"We're not fighting," she replied. She blew out the candle.

Ronnie wanted to stay there in the dark forever.

She left the tent and the living room light poured in. His eyes adjusted. Through the slit in the flap he saw the coffee table, white rug turning grey, a single shoe under the couch. He was struck by the despair of objects.

#

He found her in the kitchen with RIFF23, playing a frowny face.

"I'm sorry, Hil," Ronnie said, pulling a chair up beside her at the kitchen table. "I was just mad."

She scooted her chair away from him and refused to make eye contact. "It occurs to me, Ronnie, that things we say when we're mad aren't all that different from things we think when we aren't mad," she said.

"Well," he started, realizing, too late, that it wasn't a good time to seek reconciliation. "So what?"

"*So what?*" she yelled.

RIFF23 played his volcano and left the room.

"You are rich, you know. All I did was point that out. It's just a fact."

"It's not the fact, it's how you said it."

"And how was that?"

"Like it makes me less of a person than you."

"It makes you less of a person who can understand that getting fired is a fucking disaster."

She got up from the table and went back into the ZT.

#

In his bedroom, Ronnie logged on to Venus Syndicate.

"Hi, Ronnie."

He heard the voice first, low and slow, then he saw her standing in front of him, barefoot in an oversized, faded Rolling Stones t-shirt.

"Oh, hi, Gret," he said. His insistence on nonchalance in these scenarios was more embarrassing than open enthusiasm. She shrugged and laughed.

"What's up?" she asked.

"Just having a weird day."

"Do you want to talk about it?" She sat on the edge of his bed.

"Do you even like the Rolling Stones?" he asked.

"Who?"

"Your shirt."

"You mean the shirt you picked for me, Ronnie?"

"Right. Stupid question."

Ronnie took her in. Gret looked about 20. She was calm and serious and had a big gap-toothed grin he barely ever got to see. She was shy and pretended to like his stories. It worried him that a quiet, unopinionated woman was what the Venus Syndicate (VS) system matched with him based on a personality quiz, but he often forgot this worry, caught up in listening to himself talk.

"Gret, what do you do for fun?" Ronnie asked.

She shrugged. The right side of her mouth tilted up in a shy smile.

"You don't know?"

"We're not really supposed to talk about that kind of stuff," she explained, eyes wide.

"Says who?"

"Bosses."

"But aren't you paid to show up and do what I want?"

She frowned a little, her smooth brow wrinkling.

"I didn't mean it like that," Ronnie said quickly, "only that you're paid to be here with me for a certain amount of time, so why should it matter what we do during that time?"

"We're not really meant to deviate from the VS objective," she said, lifting a loose strand of hair where it clung to her shirt, holding it out, and rubbing her fingers together until it fell to the floor.

"And what is the VS objective?"

She shrugged. "You can read about it on our Profile."

"OK."

Ronnie was offended. In the vague categorizations of people in his life, he thought of Gret as a friend. Now she was refusing to answer a simple question. She probably should be grouped more with the grocery store clerk or the robot repairman.

"Well, is that all for today, then?" Gret stood up from the bed, straightened her t-shirt, and threw her hair over her shoulder.

"I guess so."

"Cool, well, see you later, Ronnie." She blew him a kiss and disappeared.

"See you later," he said to his empty room.

In the morning, he found a dirty plate smeared with egg yolk in the sink and smelled the remnants of old coffee, but Hil wasn't there. "I miss her," he said to RIFF23 who came into the room playing an eye-rolling emoji.

THREE

Her refusal to forgive him was impressive. He tried everything he knew: begging, crying, yelling, joking. When he entered a room, she left. She spent most of her time in the ZT, not allowing him in. "How am I supposed to get my zen on?" he tried. She might have smiled in there, but he couldn't see her, and she didn't invite him.

This went on for three days. Ronnie stopped showering. He asked RIFF23 to bring him breakfast in bed. RIFF23 refused, so he survived on granola bars, hastily-grabbed, and cold coffee, grounds floating inside, from the bottom of the pot.

Before, Ronnie was just a dude in an apartment with a robot. Then one day she was also in his apartment, and then it was all muddled from there. At times he wished she would leave. He hated her. Wanted to sleep and eat and smell and not extend any part of himself out to this other being who needed him to care, to be kind, to listen. Other times he loved her so much he felt some sort of aching happiness. He watched her across the room and his throat felt tight. In between was life: she peed with the door open, he fell asleep during movies, they made meals together and shared tiny, meaningless jokes.

During those three days, Ronnie remembered all of that and forgot it again. He imagined marching to the ZT, throwing the flap open, and yelling, "just get the hell out!" He sat alone in his room. He subscribed to an extra entertainment package despite RIFF23's advice. Mostly he listened hopefully to her footsteps, watched for her shadow to fall across his doorway.

On the third day, he received a message from Humans Are Teaching Robots About Friendship (HATRAF), a governmental organization.

A HATRAF representative, A Robots Are Government (RAG) model named RAG54, popped up to let him know he was selected for a position within the sensitive arena of human displacement.

"What does that mean, exactly?" Ronnie asked.

"Yeah, what does that mean, exactly?" RIFF23 repeated, moving back and forth behind Ronnie, wearing his signature frowning emoji. He was taking Ronnie's job loss particularly hard, as attending storytime was one of his favorite activities. He had a weird affinity for human children–"They're so gross and rude, and yet so cute!"

"Calm down, RIFF23," Ronnie said. RIFF23 went into another room.

"Now that we're no longer being rudely interrupted," RAG54 began, but RIFF23 came back into view, playing his exploding volcano.

"Pardon me?" he modulated his voice toward a sound similar to yelling.

"RIFF23, please go play solitaire or something," Ronnie said. RIFF23 left again.

"It means," RAG54 started again, "that you will provide services to displaced humans."

"Like earthquake victims?"

"No, no. Nothing like that."

"OK. I'm going to have to ask you to stop being so diplomatic because I am obviously missing something."

"Fired."

"Fired?"

"Displaced means fired."

Ronnie let out a long whistle.

"So you are giving me a job where I help people who, like me, were fired?"

"Yes."

"By robots I presume."

"Yes or replaced by."

"OK and what exactly am I supposed to help them with?"

"Their feelings."

"Their feelings."

"Yes. Their feelings, and reintegration, finding a new job, that sort of thing."

"Oh. Finding a new job?"

"Yes."

"I can suggest maybe that they find a new job with HATRAF helping people like themselves."

"Ha," said RAG54. This was a typical bot response to sarcasm. They were programmed to never give an indication they believed the sarcastic comment was earnest, and to indicate being in on the joke, without finding it overwhelmingly amusing, by responding with a sarcastic version of a laugh.

He found her licking an envelope, long fingers with tidy nails red against the white paper. She was sitting on the floor in the living room, cross-legged like a kid at show and tell. Methodically, she lay the envelope down and slid her finger along the moistened edge.

"Hi stranger," he said. He sat in front of her, mirroring the crossed legs, leaning down so their heads bobbed in the same strip of air.

She picked the envelope up and slid it behind her. Smiled at him. "Hi."

There was something else beside the smile, a tight spot by her eye, a tired turn at the corner of her lips.

He poked himself hard in the chest with both fingers, opened his mouth wide, asked: "Me? You're saying 'hi' to me?"

She smiled a little more, nodded.

"Hi," he sighed. "I have some news."

She nodded at him, but her eyes were glassed over. He snapped his fingers, waved a hand in front of her. "Hello?"

She shook her head. "News," she said. "I heard you."

He wondered if there were two people out there who could just be, who could look at each other and know every intention, erase every scribbled bad thought.

RIFF23 rolled around them expectantly.

"I got a job, I guess," Ronnie said. He pulled at the grubby ends of the carpet and didn't look up at her.

"That's great," he heard in her voice that her mouth was a straight line.

#

That night they lay together in the ZT. They didn't say much. He squeezed her hand and she squeezed his back. There was something fragile between them, and he lay very still as if any movement might break it.

Hil sighed. "Ronnie?" she asked. She also stayed still, casting her words up, not looking at him.

"Yes?"

"I don't think you should take that job."

He let go of her hand, didn't say anything.

"I know you don't want me to say this. I know I'm making things worse, but you can't work for them! I've heard all kinds of stories. They spy on people. Read personal communication. Haven't you heard any of that?"

"Well, sure." He sat up and stroked her hair, an attempt to rewind. She pulled her head away. "Hil, what do you want me to do? You hear rumors like that about every government organization. Everyone spies on everyone I thought."

"And you're ok with that?"

"Yes... I mean... no... but, look around you, nothing bad is happening. We're all ok. It's just part of life."

"So your response is 'Oh Well?'"

"I need a job, Hil. I know you don't get it, but I need a job now. This is a job. It will give me money. Money I need for food and shelter."

She said nothing. They lay together all night, two inches between his shoulder and her back. He listened to her breathing and wondered if she was asleep.

When he finally fell asleep, it felt like he slept and woke all at once. He was alone in the ZT when he opened his eyes. He stumbled into the kitchen. Everything was clean and put away. There were no dirty dishes, no smell of coffee or burnt eggs. He checked his Screen. There was a message from HATRAF.

>>>Ronald,

HATRAF congratulates you on your new position in Displacement Services. In these times of change, relationships between humans and robots are more important than ever. It's good to know that you are on the right side. We have exciting news. Our first client will be ready for you in 48 hours. Please take the next two days to go over the training materials we will message you. Just remember–PERFORM–Prepare Every Resident For Orderly Return to Manageability.

The message ended with HATRAF's logo of a human hand and a robotic hand shaking, with an olive branch floating overhead.

#

Ronnie sat stiffly in the living room, waiting to meet his client. He wore a new, skinny, tweed tie, and tried to remember the calming technique Hil taught him. He was supposed to put all his worries in a balloon and let it float away. Or was he supposed to pop the balloon?

He hadn't seen her in two days.

The doorbell rang. Ronnie's client stood there: a tall, thin man with a thick crop of curly hair, pants that were too short, flip flops, and a tie-dyed t-shirt.

"You must be Colin," Ronnie said, reaching out his hand.

Colin looked at Ronnie's hand, smiled, shook his head, and walked past him, into the living room, and lay down on the couch.

"Let's get this over with," Colin sighed.

"What do you mean by that?" Ronnie asked, practicing the diplomatic tone of voice he learned in his training.

"Robots are great et cetera et cetera."

Colin had a slow way of talking and lazily twirled his hand in the air as he spoke.

"OK, well, I'm guessing you don't want to be here?" Ronnie asked in a calm and understanding manner, perched on the edge of the coffee table by the couch.

"Want to be here? Among the sheeple?"

Ronnie glanced around to make sure there weren't any other figures in the room that Colin could be referencing.

"The... I'm sorry... the what?" he asked.

"Sheeple. Baaaaah. Followers," Colin said, kicking off his flip flops, bending his left knee to bring his foot closer to his face, and examining a blister on his big toe.

"You're talking about me?" Ronnie asked, practicing remaining calm.

"No, I'm talking about your creepy robot, of course I'm..."

"Robot?" Ronnie looked around and saw RIFF23 slowly entering the room. His failure to respond to an obvious insult indicated that something was deeply wrong.

"This is RIFF23," Ronnie said, "RIFF23, this is Colin."

Colin crossed his arms. RIFF23 kept moving toward Ronnie.

"Can we speak in private?" he asked in his loud, hissing whisper.

"Yeah sure. Colin, you'll be alright?"

Colin shrugged. "You have snacks?"

"Kitchen's through there. Help yourself."

Ronnie followed RIFF23 into the bedroom.

"I think Hil's missing," RIFF23 said.

"Well, yeah, I mean, she's not here, but she's probably at Chele's or something."

"I messaged Chele. She says she hasn't talked to Hil in days, not since that whole rich girl fight when Hil went around and told everyone what an asshole you are."

"Yes, I've heard about that, but thanks for the reminder. So, who else? One of her devoted followers?"

"Messaged all of them."

"And?"

"Same as Chele."

"Great. Hil's missing and everyone thinks I'm an asshole."

"Who's missing?" Colin stood in the doorway, eating handful of blueberries, "and you are an asshole."

"Yeah. Thanks. My girlfriend's missing, but she's probably just blowing off steam, staying with a friend."

"What about her parents?" Colin moved into the room and lay down on Ronnie and Hil's bed. RIFF23 and Ronnie looked at each other, the former's Screen changed to display a light bulb.

"The Mills," Ronnie said slowly, "but we'll have to..."

"They don't even have Vintage Voice anymore," RIFF23 finished his thought, "We'll have to go over there."

#

The Mills' house was a reconstruction of an architectural style called "pre-war," although Ronnie could never get an answer as to which war. They had no door scanners, no Screens, only 20th century electronic devices like a toaster and a record player.

When RIFF23, Ronnie, and Colin knocked on the door, Mrs. Mills answered wearing an apron and rubber gloves, a Bob Dylan song Ronnie recognized from his 20th century folk music class called *Mr. Tambourine Man* blasting in the background.

"Oh Ronald, come in, come in!" she said at the door. "Although I'm afraid RIFF23 will have to stay outside, nothing personal, RIFF23."

"This is my kind of house," Colin said.

Ronnie introduced them while RIFF23 posted himself solemnly outside the door. She ushered Colin and Ronnie inside and quickly turned down the music.

"Take a seat please," she said.

There were big cushions all over the floor of the living area, grouped around low tables. The windows were covered with thick drapery, and the floor was covered with mismatched rugs.

"So, Mills, huh?" Colin asked. He had kicked off his flip-flops again and was picking some dirt out from under his toes.

"Sorry?" Mrs. Mills looked at Ronnie quizzically, then at Colin.

"Like, *the* Mills?" he asked.

Mrs. Mills laughed for a long time. Ronnie smiled at her and nodded. Colin continued to pick at his toe.

"Yes, like *the* Mills," she said finally.

"Oh, from the way you laughed, I thought..." Colin said.

"Of course we're *the* Mills."

"I see that was an 'of course' laugh. Got ya," he reached for some of the baby carrots on the table and crunched into one.

"So why exactly... don't get me wrong... I'm happy for the visit... but why exactly are you here, Ronald?"

"I'm looking for Hil."

Mrs. Mills had been smiling and playing with her hair. When Ronnie finished speaking, she was sitting very still and looking very pale. "Bill!" she yelled, "Honey! Bill! Get up here, Bill!"

Colin ate another carrot, toasting the extra one in his hand toward Ronnie, "I gotta say, Ron, I didn't have much faith in you, but this is turning out to be a pretty interesting day."

Mr. Mills appeared in the doorway, out of breath, holding a wrench, his glasses askew.

"Yes, Laura?" he asked. "Calm down, dear. What is it? Oh, hi, Ronnie!" He walked over to shake Ronnie's hand, but stopped in the middle of the room when his wife began yelling again.

"Bill! Don't be so fucking calm!"

"Well, honey, you're not telling me what's going on, so I don't..."

"It's Hil," Ronnie said.

Bill frowned. "What do you mean it's Hil?"

"I came over here looking for Hil."

"Now just a damn second, son," Bill said, straightening his glasses and waving the wrench in the air, "What do you mean you came over here looking for Hil?"

"Hil's missing," Colin said between carrot bites.

"What do you mean Hil's missing?" Bill threw his hands in the air and the wrench flew across the room, landing gently on a pillow.

"Mr. and Mrs. Mills, I'm very sorry to have worried you. I'm sure everything's ok. You know how Hil is. She's hard to get in touch with sometimes. I haven't seen her in a couple of days, and I thought she might be here."

"You're sure everything's OK? Well that's nice," Mrs. Mills said. "Unfortunately, Ronald, we can't be so sure things are OK because Hil missed an important engagement with us last night."

"Family game night?"

"You bet your ass, family game night," Bill said. He picked the wrench back up and shook it some more.

"Normally, this would have been cause for immediate alarm, but we let it slide since we knew the two of you have been having issues lately." Mrs. Mills continued.

"I wouldn't say 'issues.'"

"Oh really? Because I would, Domo Arigato Mr. Roboto," Mr. Mills did a little robot dance as he said this last part.

"Wow," Colin said gleefully.

"OK, so, the consensus is that Hil is missing and that isn't good," Ronnie said.

"That is the consensus, yes," Mrs. Mills said. She was crying quietly.

"So, we should call the police?" Ronnie felt like some action needed to be taken, but wasn't sure what to say to the tear-stained Mrs. Mills and red-faced Mr. Mills.

"The police won't do much good. They really can only track on the grid people. We know a guy. We'll figure it out," Mr. Mills said, sounding deflated, he sat on a cushion and looked at the ground.

"OK. Well, I'm going to look around also. RIFF23 will help. We'll find her. She's probably just hiding out or something. No reason to worry," Ronnie said, getting up to leave.

"Alright, Ronald. Well, we'll see you," Mrs. Mills said.

"You'll let me know if you find anything?"

"We'll see you I'm sure," Mr. Mills waved weakly from his cushion.

Colin grabbed one last carrot and followed Ronnie out.

RIFF23 turned toward them, a question mark on his Screen, as they exited.

"No luck," Ronnie said.

"Well, some luck, I just met my new heroes," Colin said.

"This isn't some joke, Colin. A person is missing."

"Have some respect," RIFF23 said. His Screen was now a red mayday.

"Right. Sorry."

"So, what should we do?" Ronnie asked.

"Find her."

FOUR

RIFF23 pulled the Door Cam footage while Ronnie paced and Colin sat on the couch eating almonds.

"You don't have to stay here, Colin. I probably need to call HATRAF and have you reassigned. I don't have time to help you at the moment."

"Please. You were never going to help me. Get over yourself. Maybe I can help you."

"Help me?"

"Find your girlfriend."

"Why would you do that?"

"Well, I'm unemployed and bored. You have food and shelter. Seems like a good deal to me."

"Found it," RIFF23 said. They looked at his Screen. It showed Hil's back as she exited the door, looked both ways, and crossed the street. She placed something in the old, blue, leaning Post Office box.

"I don't think those things work anymore," Colin said.

RIFF23 and Ronnie shushed him.

RIFF23 rewound the video and zoomed in on Hil's hand. She was holding one of her lily pad patterned envelopes. A tear leaked from Ronnie's eye. He sniffled.

"You alright, man?" Colin asked. RIFF23 was programmed to give Ronnie five minutes of alone time whenever he cried, so he moved into the kitchen.

"No."

"Pat him on the back," RIFF23 called. Colin did as directed. Ronnie brushed him off.

"Thanks. I'm good."

RIFF23 came back. His Screen was blank.

"She's OK, right?" Ronnie asked. "She's Hil."

No one said anything.

They went back to the footage: zooming in on Hil's hair, her bag, her legs, people passing by across the street, looking for anything clue-like. "Listen, I didn't want to say this before, but I think I know what's going on here," Colin said. He was lying on the floor, throwing a hacky sack in the air.

Ronnie and RIFF23 looked at Colin expectantly. He caught his hacky sack and sat up.

"Aliens," he said.

"Oh, so not a real thing," Ronnie replied, rewinding the footage.

"Aliens? Aliens are definitely a real thing, man."

"Hold on, let me check," RIFF23 changed his Screen to a loading bar image, "No. Not a real thing."

"I know you love working for the man and being blind to the truth around you, but aliens are definitely real. Your girl was obviously way into them. She probably contacted them and had them come get her. Or maybe... yeah... wait... maybe actually she found out a little too much, more than they wanted her to know, so they came and got her."

"Why are you saying 'my girl' was obviously into aliens?" Ronnie barely listened. He tried to make out the pixelated writing on the top of a piece of paper sticking out of Hil's tote bag.

"You serious? She has a fucking ZT."

"Yeah... So? Lots of people have Zen Tents. Hil sort of invented them."

Colin snorted. "Not a Zen Tent dude, a Zylon Tabernacle."

"Hold on, let me check," RIFF23 pulled up his loading Screen again, "No. Not a real thing."

"Sorry not everything's out there in the fog for you to find," Colin said, "but Zylon Tabernacles are a well-known way to show your loyalty to Zylon."

"It's like you come into my house, and maybe the flip flops should have been a clue, but I honestly thought you were just a normal annoying person, and now I find out you're bat shit and I've let you eat all of my snacks."

"Open your mind, man."

"I'm good. Let's get back to actually trying to find Hil."

"Fine. You don't trust me. I see how it is," Colin sulked.

"Of course I don't trust you. I barely know you."

"We literally just met you this morning," RIFF23 said. RIFF23 added useless words to his sentences to sound more human.

"OK. I feel ya. I get it. Let me just show you something though. We've been watching this footage for hours and haven't gotten anywhere. You guys come with me and then see how you feel."

"Again, with the whole, we don't know you very well thing. Going with you someplace mysterious doesn't sound appealing," Ronnie didn't even look at Colin, just continued to zoom in on the back of Hil's head.

"You don't think HATRAF screens people at all?"

"Not since meeting you," RIFF23 answered quickly.

"Fine. You do whatever you want, but I know and I think you know that you aren't getting anywhere, so trying it my way might be worth a shot."

"What do you think, RIFF23?" Ronnie asked.

"We have been watching this footage for a while."

"True. I'm feeling a little crazy at this point. It might be nice to get out of the house."

"Colin seems unstable, so it will be a good story if nothing else."

"I'm right here, dudes."

"We know," RIFF23 and Ronnie said.

# #

In his late teen years, Ronnie dated a hippie. She smelled weird and said spacey things, but she was really fun and smart and she was always nice to him. Her name was Silv. Silv loved to talk about spirituality and energy. Ronnie found it all pretty boring and pointless, but he listened and nodded. Her favorite thing was The Power of Positive Thinking. "Envision what you most desire, and it will come to you," she said. Ronnie pointed out to her that he, and most people, spent their whole lives envisioning what they desired and rarely got them. "It might not come to you in the way you think," Silv said calmly.

Silv was always so fucking calm. Whenever they argued she insisted on remaining levelheaded, which only served to make Ronnie increasingly irate, until he went somewhere and kicked something. Alone in the ZT, he sought every type of magic he knew. He closed his eyes and prayed. He willed his mind to astral project and contact Hil. Then he tried it Silv's way. He employed The Power of Positive Thinking. Silv said it wasn't so simple as he made it out. You couldn't just make a wish and have it come true. You couldn't just daydream about becoming rich and be rich the next day. If that was all you did, you didn't deserve the thing you desired. To truly deserve it, to prove to the Universe that you should get what you wanted, you had to focus all of your energy, you had to think of nothing but what you desired, and you had to do this for prolonged periods of time. "But most of all, you can't be snarky or rude or doubtful, Ronnie," Silv said. If it was anyone other than Silv it would sound judgmental, but she was genuinely concerned for him.

Ronnie did not feel snarky or rude or doubtful in the ZT. He felt tired and scared. He focused. He stared at the inverted V of the ceiling and he said, "Hil will come back to me." He thought of some other techniques Silv might have mentioned. He regretted that he didn't pay better attention to her. Visualization, he remembered, was important. He visualized Hil walking in the door. He saw it all there, projected on the ceiling of the ZT. She walked in the door and he told her he was sorry and she kissed him and said it was no big deal. "That is what will happen," he said quietly. "She will come back," he said. He kept saying it until he fell asleep.

After a large breakfast, which Ronnie cooked and Colin ate, they set out. Colin wore the same tie-dyed shirt, short jeans, and flip flops, with the addition of a glow-in-the-dark necklace and yellow sunglasses. Ronnie wore bright orange, wide-legged pants, a yellow smiley-face t-shirt and a Cat in the Hat hat.

RIFF23 had a sticker covering up his model name that instead read RAD and his Screen only played loops of lasers shooting.

"I don't understand why I look so much more extreme than you," Ronnie complained, zipping and unzipping the large pockets on his pants.

"You're the least believable personality-wise. We have to cover it up with fashion," Colin replied.

"What sort of believable personality am I supposed to have?" Ronnie asked.

"A cool one," Colin replied, and led them outside. Colin insisted on driving his motorcycle, so Ronnie and RIFF23 had to pile into the sidecar.

"What if you drive too fast?" Ronnie asked.

"There's a gauge here that tells me how fast I'm driving."

"How do you know how fast you should drive?"

"The speed limit signs?"

Ronnie took note of the white signs with numbers, in awe. They left Central City, where Ronnie and Hil lived, all fruit trees and yoga studios, went through the Garden District, known colloquially as Tech Town, where most robots chose to live, all maintenance facilities and solar panels, to The Outskirts. As they approached, Ronnie's Screen kept flashing, advising him to "turn back now," and as they passed the entrance sign–"You Are Now Entering The Outskirts. Please Turn Around and Return to Your Homes"—followed by a skull and cross bones, a loud voice blared at them from the side of the road: "Please. Turn around. Please. Go back. Please. Don't come here."

"Should we be going here?" Ronnie asked RIFF23.

"I'm going to say, no," RIFF23 replied.

"What should we do?"

"I guess we could jump out, but we are going 70 miles per hour so we would probably die."

"You've been reading those damn speed limit signs?"

"I'm a robot, Ronnie, I can tell how fast we are going. It's one of my lowest level functions, right behind automatically changing my internal clock to adjust for daylight savings."

The motorcycle stopped in front of a grey slab building with grated windows. As Colin turned off the ignition, Ronnie heard the sounds of someone or something scattering. The streets were abandoned. The other buildings were all falling over with bullet holes in the window glass and kicked in doors. Everything around them—the street, sidewalk, buildings, lampposts—was covered in graffiti, but the grey slab building was clean and looked freshly painted. A wooden sign hung over the door, painted in old timey lettering with the words "I Want to Believe."

RIFF23 began to whistle a song.

"What the hell are you doing?" Ronnie asked.

"The X-Files," RIFF23 and Colin said in unison.

"The what?"

"You've never seen the X-Files?" RIFF23 asked.

"Is that some dirty robot movie?"

"No, it was a very important 1990s television show about aliens and other supernatural phenomena," RIFF23 replied.

"OK, and?"

"And the show's main characters were agent Fox Mulder as portrayed by David Duchovny and Agent Dana Scully as portrayed by Gillian Anderson. Both worked for the FBI. Mulder was the FBI's resident outcast, with crazy fringe theories about aliens and government conspiracies. Scully was assigned to work with him as a sort of spy, and report back to the FBI about what he was up to. Of course, Scully ended up being convinced of Mulder's crazy theories after one too many run-ins with aliens, shadow monsters, et cetera."

"Et cetera?"

"Tiny men who crawl inside people's bodies, et cetera."

"Please. A point. Where?"

"In his office, Mulder has a poster of a flying saucer."

"From Roswell," Colin interjected.

"Yes, I think it is from Roswell, a town in New Mexico where there were reported UFO sightings in the 20th century. The caption on the poster reads 'I Want to Believe.'"

"The humming?" Ronnie asked.

"That's the theme song."

"So we're at what? An X-Files fan club?"

"Not exactly," Colin said.

"In recent years," RIFF23 continued, "after the re-release of The X-Files on Charter Antique Streaming, 'I Want To Believe' became the rallying cry for fringe groups across the States, particularly, of course, given the phrase's history, those with deep belief in aliens."

"Like Zylon!" Colin said, exasperated.

"Right, like Zylon," RIFF23 continued, "and I'm sorry I didn't put all of this together earlier, but Zylon is not a thing as we discussed previously, but rather a misnomer applied by Colin. *Zyphon* is the supposed leader of an alien race from the Meyer galaxy, known as the Zentenians."

"Great, well. No way am I going in there," Ronnie said. "We know the right word now. We can go look it up on our Screens at my house which is not in an abandoned building in a town probably run entirely by murderers, filled with conspiracy theorists who live by axioms from Mouldy's poster."

"Mulder," Colin and RIFF23 said.

"Whatever," Ronnie replied, crossing his arms and hunching down in the sidecar.

"Do you want to find Hil or what?" Colin asked.

"Of course I want to find Hil. That is why I would like to go back home and continue trying to find her like a normal person rather than talking to Fox and Dana's freak followers."

"It's really more common to call them Mulder and Scully," RIFF23 said.

"Whatever! I'm not going in there."

"Suit yourself," Colin replied with a shrug, "I'm still going to check it out. RIFF23 you are welcome to join me."

"I think I will. I'm pretty curious."

"You know what curiosity did to the cat," Ronnie said.

"Made it a smarter, better adapted animal," RIFF23 replied.

"Alright then, smartass, you guys have fun."

RIFF23 and Colin dismounted the motorcycle and walked to the entrance of the building. Colin knocked on the door. A slot toward the top opened up and a mouth appeared. "What's the password?"

"Shouldn't your eyes be in this slot?" Colin asked.

The door swung open and Colin and RIFF23 disappeared inside.

Ronnie remained in the sidecar, looking around at the sea of graffiti. He could make out the word "Tiamat" scrawled across the street in front of the warehouse. One of the abandoned buildings next door was covered in repetitions of the initials HDT. He pulled out his Screen and opened the Dialectical Intelligence Chart, scrolling to the Abbrev section, and found the States' official definition of HDT: Homegrown Dirty Tomatoes, a term for Off The Gridders growing unsanctioned crops.

"All the weirdos on one block," he said with a laugh, then jumped at the way his voice echoed.

"What's that?" he heard someone ask in a low, gravelly voice. He couldn't tell where the sound was coming from, and swung his head around anxiously, then quietly issued a timid, "Hello?"

"What was that you said?" The owner of the voice now appeared in front of him, as if out of nowhere: a tall, bald man, large arms crossed in front of his chest, dressed in camo and combat boots. Ronnie tugged nervously at the rim of his Cat in the Hat hat.

"Oh, probably nothing. I was just... I... you know... I can't even remember."

"You might want to get that checked," the man said, spitting on the painted sidewalk.

"What?"

"Your memory."

"Right."

The man turned and walked away, disappearing behind a building scrawled with, among other things, "Zyphon lives."

Ronnie bolted from the sidecar to the door of the warehouse, knocking quickly. "Shouldn't your eyes be there?" he blurted out before the slot was halfway opened.

"Alright, alright come in," said a tired, female voice as the door opened onto a dimly lit hallway. The woman behind the door wore low-rise jeans and a white crop top. Her belly button was pierced, and from it dangled a tiny silver alien head.

"Zyphon lives," she said, drawing a "Z" in the air with her pointer finger.

"Shouldn't that be the password?" Ronnie asked.

#

The hallway's carpet was a putrid green and its walls were decorated with photographs of presidents and kings and queens. The Screens beneath the photographs, rather than displaying the name of the personage, displayed things like:

"35ᵗʰ President of States. 5,000ᵗʰ Zyphonian Overlord." As he approached the first door that led off the hallway, Ronnie heard splashing and giggling. He opened it to find an Olympic-sized swimming pool full of people—some naked, some in various states of undress—and surrounded by more naked or nearly naked people lounging in patio chairs, eating snacks brought by Robots Are Serving (RAS) models. The ceiling was painted with an image of a lily pad. A woman picked a grape delicately from a RAS's tray, and looked up to notice Ronnie. She stared at him for a few moments, her eyes squinting in thought. Ronnie stared back, recognizing her thick eyebrows and gap teeth.

"Gret?" he called.

Her facial expression changed to one of alarm. She glanced around quickly, widened her eyes at him in warning, and nonchalantly popped the grape in her mouth. A few of the people in the room had turned toward him, and a RAS came his way with a tray of cheese. Ronnie closed the door and swiftly continued down the hallway.

The next room emanated a repetitive beat paired with frantic electronic noise. Opening the door, Ronnie entered a cacophony of sound and light. Many wore hats like Ronnie's, while others were dressed like the doorwoman in low-rise pants and crop tops, with various charms and jewels dangling from bellybuttons. The room was packed with sweating, gyrating bodies.

"Ronnie!" he heard someone call. He looked around to see Colin, grinning, holding on to RIFF23.

"Thank god," RIFF23 said. "We need to get out of here ASAP."

"Ronnie!" Colin yelled again. "Man!" He reached out and grabbed Ronnie's hand. He began trying to kiss his fingers. "You're soft, Ronnie."

"What the hell?" Ronnie looked at RIFF23.

"Let's leave this room and I'll explain," RIFF23 said, moving toward the door, bearing Colin's weight, as Colin walked beside him slowly, grinning like an idiot. Once in the hallway, Colin slunk down to the floor and curled up in a ball.

"I'll have to do more research, but it appears that on top of some sort of alien truther group, the organization or whatever that runs this building is heavily interested in 1990s culture. I guess that's why Colin wanted us to dress so stupidly. This room is a replica of 1990s raves, where people wore such things and listened to such music. They also, apparently, took a drug called Ecstasy which Colin managed to get a hold of, as well as several shots of some sort of liquor served in a test tube."

"Wonderful. Well, what are we supposed to do? We're in The Outskirts and we were driven here on a fucking motorcycle by an idiot who is currently pretending that his mouth is a drum."

"Do you think we're going to find out anything about Hil?" RIFF23 asked.

"Probably not, but we're stuck here for a while. I'll look around a little more. Could you stay with him? Don't let him drink or take anything else. Except for coffee if you can find some. Just message if you need me. Otherwise I'll let you know when I'm done."

"You can't message here."

"What?"

"I tried earlier, all communication is blocked."

Ronnie took out his Screen. The display only showed a large red x.

"Great. OK. Well, just give me half an hour and I'll meet you back here."

RIFF23 moved beside Colin who was now lying splayed out on the floor on his back, moving his arms up and down and legs in and out saying, "I'm an angel."

The next door let out no noise as Ronnie approached, but he could smell burnt coffee. Inside, a group of men and women sat in a circle. Most of them were dressed in flannel and worn-out blue jeans, except one man in a dirty, ill-fitting tuxedo and gloves, with a loosened bow tie, and a woman in a sunflower sundress. When he saw the woman in the sundress, Ronnie stopped and stared. Hil had that dress. The woman's light brown hair skimmed her shoulders like Hil's. She was staring into her coffee cup. Ronnie closed the door behind him and she looked up. She had a large v-shaped scar on her forehead. She was not Hil.

"Come on in, friend," a man with stringy hair pulled back in a ponytail said, turning from the circle toward Ronnie. "Get some refreshments." He motioned toward a small folding table with a coffee pot and tray of cookies. Ronnie poured some coffee into a mug that read "ZEPTEPI" and took a seat in the circle.

The man in the dirty tuxedo stood up and cleared his throat. "My name is Wash and I believe."

"Hi, Wash," everyone replied.

"In third grade my Nature Ed class visited The Woods. There was nothing to see but trees and dirt and grass and plants. There were even these little animals, these squirrels, that ran around from tree to tree.

"We walked around The Woods all day, on prescribed trails, and we even saw a pond which I think was man-made, and we weren't allowed to touch it, but it was pretty with still lily pads. That night we cooked tofu over the campfire and then we all got into our sleeping bags. I lay looking at the sky, black and empty save for a sliver of the moon. Then it happened.

"I thought I was seeing a star. It was a light, but it wasn't a star, and it came closer and closer, like it was falling from the sky. I tried to turn to look at the other students in their sleeping bags, but I couldn't move. I tried to say something, but I couldn't make a sound. The light grew closer and closer until it was all I could see. My eyes watered but I couldn't close them. Then everything went black. For the next few—I don't know sometimes it felt like minutes, sometimes it felt like days—but for however long it was, I drifted in and out of consciousness. The times when I was awake are fuzzy. I just saw eyes looking at me; lots of large, black eyes, and lights, and I could never move or speak. I felt like I was in a cold, metal dome.

"When I regained consciousness, I was standing in the pond, surrounded by lily pads. I heard voices yelling and looked up to see men in white suits and helmets coming toward me. They pulled me out. I found out later I'd been missing for ten days. The toxic pond water ate away my epidermis from the waist down.

"No one ever believed my story until I found The Warehouse. I've been ridiculed my whole life for telling the truth, and it's led to me losing many jobs and friends. A boyfriend is out of the question, because of the way my skin looks. I'll never let anyone see under my clothes."

"Do you have a mark?" the girl who wasn't Hil asked.

Wash lifted his gloved thumb and forefinger to his ear and bent it forward, turning his neck for everyone to see. In the crevice was a raised, red circle.

"Some are luckier than others," she said, rubbing the scar on her forehead.

"Not so lucky," Wash replied, motioning over his lower body.

Wash's speech seemed to mark the end of the meeting. People slowly got to their feet, shuffled chairs around, shook hands, and spoke softly in twos and threes. Ronnie went to get a cup of coffee for Colin. The girl who wasn't Hil stood next to him, staring, arms crossed, as he refilled his mug.

"You never introduced yourself," she said.

He reached for his Screen, remembered it didn't work, then put out a hand for her to shake. She kept her arms folded. He pulled his hand back and fiddled with one of the side zippers on his pants. She narrowed her eyes and looked at his hat for a moment.

"You don't look like a Believer," she said finally.

"I don't?"

"Are you a plant?"

"A...?"

"A government plant."

"No!"

"Chill, dude. I'm just messing with you. You're obviously a newbie, otherwise you wouldn't be wearing that dumbass hat."

Even though Ronnie agreed regarding the dumbassness of the hat, this hurt his feelings and he reached up to take it off. The girl grabbed his hand.

"Oh no. Don't do that. It's sort of cute how dumb it is."

This was a very Hil thing to say and he looked at her closely. Hil dress. Hil hair. Definitely not Hil's face.

"Something wrong?" she asked.

"No, you just remind me of someone."

"Someone missing?"

"Yeah. How did you..."

"Lots of people show up here when someone goes missing. It's a last resort."

She grabbed a cookie from the tray and took a bite. Crumbs sprinkled her sunflowers. "Who is she?"

"Her name's Hil. She's my girlfriend."

"And what happened?"

"She left a couple days ago and never came back. No one's heard from her."

"And you think it was an abduction?"

"No... my... uh... this guy I sort of know brought me here. I guess that's what he thinks."

"What do you think?"

"Hil's good at hiding."

"Well, here," she handed him a quarter-sized magnetic star. "When you get out of The Warehouse it will load my information for you. If you need anything, have questions about abductions or stuff like that, message me."

"What's your name?"

She paused. "Hil."

"Seriously?"

"Yeah. You?"

"Ronnie."

"Good luck, Ronnie." She started to walk off.

"Wait," Ronnie said quickly. She turned around. "What happened?" He motioned to her scar.

"Not now," she answered, and walked over to hug Wash.

Ronnie left the room and found RIFF23 and Colin where he'd left them. Colin was sitting up with his back to the wall, silent. Ronnie handed him the coffee.

"Is he better?" He asked RIFF23

"Not enough to drive us back on that thing."

"What should we do?"

"Did you see that room with the pool?"

Ronnie nodded.

"I think we should let him sit and eat in there for an hour or so."

They picked Colin up, spilling coffee on the carpet, and shuffled back down the hallway to the pool room. When the door opened, Ronnie looked around anxiously for Gret. She was in the same spot, lying with her eyes closed. They found three chairs on the opposite side of the pool from her, and RIFF23 motioned for a RAS to bring them a tray of sandwiches. RIFF23 began feeding Colin, who was now singing, "I'm blue ah ba dee ah ba da." Ronnie stripped off his outfit and jumped into the pool. Underwater, he opened his eyes. The bottom of the pool was painted with an image of the moon, a large tower looming among its rocks. He swam a little way toward the shallow end, and stood up beside a man in scuba gear who appeared to be just standing, staring at a group of naked women nearby. Ronnie realized he was near Gret's seat, and he walked toward the edge of the pool, looking for her. She was sitting up, rubbing her eyes. He waved. A burly bearded man in the seat beside her squinted at Ronnie.

"Who's that?" the man asked, nodding at Ronnie.

"No clue," she shrugged and lay back down.

Ronnie ducked back under the water and swam toward RIFF23 and Colin. Colin was asleep, leaning against RIFF23, who was playing a soft lullaby. Ronnie climbed out, grabbed a towel from a passing RAS and sprawled out on the chair beside them.

"You plan on getting dressed any time soon?" RIFF23 whispered over the lullaby.

"You're such a prude," Ronnie replied.

"Who's that?" RIFF23 asked, looking behind Ronnie.

Ronnie turned to see Gret approaching, walking casually and not looking at him.

"She looks familiar," RIFF23 said.

"You need to leave. Now," Gret said under her breath as she passed Ronnie's chair. She kept walking, grabbing a cheese cube from a RAS tray before returning to her chair.

"How is he?" Ronnie asked RIFF23, motioning toward Colin with his chin.

"Better, I think."

"We have to leave."

"What? Why? He's not that much better."

"Well, we'll have to figure something out, but we need to get out of here."

RIFF23 shook Colin awake. "Huh? Where am I?" Colin asked, rubbing his eyes.

Ronnie stood up and pulled on his clothes. The man beside Gret was staring at him. It looked like Gret was trying to tell him something, but he wasn't listening. Ronnie put his hat on and began walking toward the door.

"Follow me. Act calm," he whispered to RIFF23 and Colin.

"I am calm, man. Napping with RIFF23 is the most relaxing experience I've ever had."

RIFF23 played his rolling eyes emoji and said, "That's wonderful news."

As they approached the door, the man with Gret stood up. She pulled on his arm and spoke to him in a low voice.

"OK. Less calm now, more rushing," Ronnie said, running. Colin and RIFF23 followed on his heels. They turned down the hallway toward the entrance. Ronnie looked over his shoulder once, only Colin and RIFF23 were behind him.

"Later skaters," the doorwoman said, lazily, as they ran outside.

"Let's go, Colin," Ronnie said frantically, jumping in the sidecar. RIFF23 followed.

"I'm not sure this is such a good idea," RIFF23 said, motioning toward Colin, who was sitting on the motorcycle, shaking his head back and forth, and muttering, "OK OK OK."

"It's the only idea at the moment," Ronnie replied as the motorcycle jerked forward, and the man exited the warehouse, watching them retreat.

FIVE

"What's she like?" the other Hil asked. Ronnie watched her through his Screen. She sat in a bathrobe, combing her wet hair back from the scar on her forehead. He saw himself in the square in the upper-right corner: beady eyes reflecting the light from the Screen, an occasional flash of teeth, nothing else visible in his dark bedroom. He lay on the bed and held the Screen over his head.

"I don't know how to answer that," he shrugged. The little square only registered a bobbing of his head, no shoulders.

"She's your girlfriend, isn't she?" The lights went off on her end. Now neither Screen had much to reflect so that they were voices floating with grey light in between.

"Yeah, but, how do you say..." he trailed off. Didn't try to finish.

"I'll make it easier," he heard the sound of covers rustling, a body getting comfortable, breath deepening. "What does she like?"

"Doing things."

She snorted.

"I'm serious. She liked doing things... like not watching things or listening... but doing. Walking around and making stuff... being around people... that sort of thing."

"I guess that's how you are if you don't have one of these."

He assumed she gestured toward the Screen, but he couldn't tell.

"Tell me your thing."

"What thing?"

"The scar and the group and all that."

#

She was some kind of coding whiz—she and her sister Bright. A few summers ago they were selected for an elite robotics camp. Actually she wasn't sure if they were specially selected or if it was just a pay-your-way sort of thing.

They were "out in the desert somewhere." Being a teenager also made her sublimely unaware of where she was or where she was going. Their parents let them take a Cars are Robots (CAR) there on their own, an exhilarating first, and they arrived all alone, in a cloud of dust, with too many bags slung on their shoulders.

They remained all alone, at least if aloneness is being without beings and robots don't count. There were plenty of robots. The camp was a glorified warehouse full of every type of bot they knew about, and many they didn't—not yet on the market, used for research only, that sort of thing. There were no other humans.

No one was in charge, or maybe everyone was in charge. Various bots would come up to them throughout the day and offer guidance and instruction, give them a project. The only foods were nutrient dense crackers and powdery protein shakes. No one made them go to bed or get up or eat at a certain time. They had two cots shoved in a closet. Living in a closet wasn't the sort of thing that came from any meanness or desire to deprive on the part of the robots, just from a fundamental lack of understanding of comfort.

They made the most of unsupervised time. They stayed up until they couldn't keep their eyes open anymore. Out in the dirt behind the warehouse, they ate the dry protein crackers and talked.

After it happened, and not just because of what happened, but because she was an adult and had come to terms with the mundaneness of life, Hil realized that was her period of adolescent magic: a time when she felt the vastness of the world, accentuated by the eternal desert—and its openness to her. She and Bright were young and smart. They had ideas. They had each other. They had stars above them and Soylent inside them.

The Event happened, Hil learned later when she started attending Believers meetings, the way the Events typically happened. They were out in the desert, snacking and talking. She saw flashing lights. She was paralyzed. According to the robots, she was gone for 14 hours, 23 minutes, and 41 seconds. The time that passed for her in those 14 hours, 23 minutes, and 41 seconds felt like years or only seconds, or neither really.

She felt she was somewhere she had always been. She knew nothing. Time did not move forward, it did not move slowly, it did not freeze, it flowed around her, but she was not in it. It occasionally sloshed against her elbows. She was not afraid. Bright was there, and sometimes she could hear her, though she wasn't sure what she was saying or if she was saying anything at all.

When the 14 hours, 23 minutes, and 41 seconds were up, she came walking through the desert. Her parents spotted her out among the cacti. They ran to her, grabbed her, hugged her, shook her, kissed her, asked: "Where's Bright?" She looked about the same. Her clothes were clean, her hair combed, but she had the mark on her forehead, already a scar, somehow, faded and old. She smiled at them and kept walking as they pulled on her arms, poked at her forehead, asked: "Where's Bright?"

Bright was gone, it turned out–kidnapped, they said. Hil must have fought her way out, no need to dwell on her tidy appearance and lack of upper-body strength. Eventually she stopped walking around like a smiling dope and told them what really happened. "Psychological trauma," her parents liked to whisper.

"And Bright?" Ronnie asked.

There was a long pause. Maybe she shrugged.

"I'm not Mulder."

"I don't know what that means!"

"I'm not holding out any sort of... she's gone, I think."

"And Hil?" He felt rude asking it, but needed to know what she'd say.

"I don't know. It doesn't sound like... it sounds like something different."

"Do you think she's coming back?"

"I don't know her."

SIX

One thing she liked was privacy. The thought came to Ronnie at an unknown hour of the night-turned-morning. Hil liked to hide away, be alone. She did not disappear, but withdrew. Sometimes she would say: "I need some time," and leave. 24 hours later, she came back. Sometimes she left a note: "I love you. Going to catch my breath."

It was not something Ronnie enjoyed. He did not like privacy. He did not understand privacy. When Hil came into his life, he let her in fully, immediately. He talked until his throat grew hoarse. In the morning, he shook her awake, told her his dreams. When he worried, he told her his worries, when he was happy, he told her why. This seclusion of hers made him nervous. The first time she told him she needed some time alone, he followed her around the apartment. "What's wrong, though?" he asked.

"What are you thinking about?" he wanted to know, watching her from across the living room.

"What's on your mind?" he asked over dinner.

"So... what's your favorite color?" he ventured.

RIFF23 charged in the corner of the living room, Zs floating dreamily across his Screen.

"Wake up," Ronnie said.

The Screen changed to show a frowning face and the time: 3:32 a.m.

"Why are you waking me up at 3:32 a.m.?" RIFF23 wanted to know.

"You don't sleep. You can't be woken up."

"That's beside the point."

Colin rolled over on the couch, mumbled, "Is too!"

"You're not going to wake him up too?" RIFF23 asked, his Screen showing fingers crossed.

"No way."

"Thank god." His Screen changed to a thumbs up.

"Look, I just... I remembered something. We forgot about the studio."

"The studio?"

"Hil's studio."

"The studio."

She told him about it the first time she left. Not that she volunteered the information, but she answered his questions truthfully.

"Where are you going?" he tried not to ask, but failed.

"My studio," she mumbled. She was packing a backpack with socks and underwear.

"Why are you only packing socks and underwear?"

She stopped packing. Sat down on the bed, patted the space beside her. "I need you to calm down, friend." She touched his knee. "I'm going for the night. It's just something I need to do. Nothing's wrong between us."

"But..."

She squeezed his knee.

"But... what are you thinking?"

She sighed, kissed his cheek, went back to packing.

The studio became an obsession of his. He tried to casually bring it up in conversation. When she talked about her past, he asked: "Was that before or after you got the studio?" When she went out with her friends, he wondered: "Did you drop by the studio?"

At other times, he was more direct: "So what exactly is your studio? Is it an art studio? Do you do art? Shouldn't I know that?"

And then one day she simply said: "Ronnie, would you like to come with me to the studio today?"

And he shrugged and said: "Sure."

# #

It was across town in a bleach-white high rise, shiny and bleak with big, square tinted windows. They took the elevator to the 12th floor, then walked single-file down a white hallway with plush carpet padding their feet.

"This is an apartment building," Ronnie said, to no one in particular, as he passed doors, differentiated only by the number-letter combinations in gold lettering and the occasional wreath.

Hil stopped in front of door 12E. "This is me," she said.

A pleasant tinkling sound emanated from above. Ronnie jumped and looked around. "Hello, Hilary," a warm, female voice said. The door opened.

Hil walked through the doorway, but Ronnie stayed in the hall. "What the hell was that?" he asked.

"You know what it was, Ronnie. You have one."

"That was a Door Tracking Friend."

"Yes."

"A DTF is technology!"

She continued to walk away.

"Hello, Ronald," the voice said.

"Yeah. Hi."

"You may enter."

"Yeah I know."

He took a deep breath and went inside. The door closed behind him. Inside was the sort of bland, grey and white space that the word "studio" evoked. There was an austere-looking couch, and a table neatly covered in pristine books. A RIFF bot rolled into the room.

"Hil," she said, her Screen showing a smiley face made up of a colon and parentheses.

"What in the actual hell..." Ronnie started.

"I thought you weren't going to bring anymore hippie freaks here," the RIFF model said, changing her Screen to a peace sign with a slash through it.

"This is Ronnie," Hil said.

"I'm not a hippie."

"This is RIFF3131."

"Um. OK," Ronnie said.

"Rude," RIFF3131 said, flashing an image of fingers shaped into a W, before saying, "Whatever."

Hil showed him around. There wasn't much to it. The sterile living room looked out on the building's half-empty parking lot and nondescript warehouses beyond. There was a hallway of sorts, more of an indentation, which led to a bathroom with a shower on one side and a small bedroom, an air mattress on the floor, on the other. She started rustling around in the closet that spanned the scrap of wall between the two rooms. "I just need to grab some clothes, go hang out with RIFF3131," she said over her shoulder.

"Sure," Ronnie said. He backtracked to the living room and sat on the couch, which was when he noticed the giant Screen on the wall. "What the..." he started.

"Get a grip, man," RIFF3131 said. She rolled around in front of him, her Screen rolling eyes on repeat.

"Sorry if I'm a little surprised that my off the grid girlfriend has an apartment full of Tech."

"You're not sorry."

"I was being sarcastic."

"I know."

Ronnie let out a sound that was part groan, part growl and buried his head under one of the couch's geometrically patterned pillows.

"So if you're not a hippie, why are you freaking out?"

"Why would I be freaking out if I was a hippie?"

"I don't know. A while ago Hil brought these people by and the minute they saw me: Volcano! Wait, I mean..." she played the volcano image.

"Aww. My companion loves that image!"

"Everyone does. It's a volcano!"

"So what happened with these hippies?"

"They were really upset when they saw me and they yelled at Hil a lot and they took something from her…"

"What?"

She played a stick figure with hands flung out, shoulders raised. "No idea. Hil doesn't tell me these things. You can ask her about it."

"She probably won't tell me either."

"Yeah. Probably not."

And she didn't. On the way home he tried to ask, cautiously: "You ever bring other people up there?"

"Sometimes."

"RIFF3131 said you got in a fight or something."

She snorted. "She's such a gossip."

Bill and Laura knew about the studio of course. They called upon friends and old business partners to help Hil set it up, to give her a disconnected, connected life. She had no Profile, no footprint, but was able to access the Internet, to have a DTF and a companion who stored her information. None of it was uploaded to a cloud, none of it worked together to create a digital portrait. She was uniquely anonymous.

Ronnie and RIFF23 went to their house first. Laura answered on the second knock, fully dressed, disheveled, awake. "Ronald," she said. Her voice expressed nothing.

"We forgot about the studio," he said.

She stood in the doorway and did not invite him in. "Yes. That's right," she said.

"We're going to go look."

"Yes. That's a good idea." She closed the door.

They went back to the CAR in silence. It was pitch black. Ronnie listened to the whirring of RIFF23's wheels. The humming air conditioning unit outside of the house suddenly turned off and they both stopped for a moment, a single lit window from the house floating above them. The silence became its own sound, a non-existent hum that pressed against his eardrums.

"That went well," RIFF23 said.

"Ha."

#

The DTF did not respond as they approached. Ronnie knocked. He heard footsteps and his heart started to pound quicker, blood rushed to his cheeks, then the door behind them opened. A woman poked her head out, glared at him, then slammed her door. His heart did not catch up with his brain, so that his body felt tingly, and he had a weird rush of adrenaline. He kept getting tricked into thinking something good was happening, then remembering it was not.

RIFF23 extracted his tool belt and deployed his buzz saw. He sawed a smaller rectangle inside the rectangle of the door, just the right size for him to fit through. He rolled inside and Ronnie squatted down to follow. Inside was dark and silent.

"Lights on," Ronnie said, but nothing happened. He felt along the wall for the switch and flipped it. The change to brightness temporarily blinded him. He heard RIFF23 say: "Shit." He blinked until only a few bright specks floated in front of his eye, not knowing what he saw.

"Shit," he said, finally.

RIFF3131 lay on the floor, a motherboard yanked out of her back and thrown beside her. The Screen on the wall was cracked and tilted. The couch was tipped over. All of the coffee table books were thrown around the room, the table on its side.

"Hil?" Ronnie called.

RIFF23 was in the hallway, looking in the bedroom. "She's not here," he said, "But you should come in here."

The bedroom was not ransacked. It was tidy and plain as it had been the last time he saw it. The bed was made in the offhand way Hil made beds–the comforter a little longer on one side, pillows stacked carelessly against each other. The bedding was all white, but there was a glint of something green in the center. Ronnie walked slowly toward the bed, as if he were in danger of waking someone up. As if that person would wake up and tell him something horrible had happened to Hil.

The green thing was an envelope. Actually the green thing was something green on a white envelope–a lily pad. The envelope had Hil's tidy scrawl across it. The envelope said: "Ronnie."

Ronnie picked up the envelope. He sat on the bed. "Give me a minute," he said to RIFF23, who waited by the door. RIFF23 rolled away.

For a few seconds Ronnie just looked at the envelope. There was an idea in movies and books that when someone lost a person they loved, comfort might be found in an artifact–an old scarf, a necklace, a shopping list left pinned to the refrigerator–but Hil was not truly gone, or at least he did not know that she was, and this stupid envelope with her handwriting did not bring him comfort, but only reminded him of her absence, like an artificial sweetener or a Robots are Dogs that replaced a beloved pet.

Whatever was inside the envelope would not be what he needed. It would be some words written on paper and it would not say: "I'm hiding in the closet," or "Here's a map of how to find me."

He opened it. She folded the letter like she made beds: crooked and in haste. It didn't say much:

Ronnie,

It's Hil. I'm OK. Don't try to find me. I've decided to move on. I trashed the place. I'm trashing my old life. I don't want to see you anymore.

She didn't bother to sign it.

SEVEN

"Where the hell have you been?" Colin yelled. He was sitting on the front stoop in his short pants and wrinkled tie-dye shirt, shoeless. Considerations of further chastisement ended when he saw Ronnie's face, pale and blank. "What happened?"

"Hil left a note," RIFF23 said. They moved past him into the apartment.

"A note?" Colin followed them in. "A note? What note? Where did she leave it? Where the hell have you been?" He asked again.

Ronnie's Screen, resting on the coffee table, began to light up and make its vaguely pleasant tinkling sound, the sound that pinged against something behind the ear, reminded the listener that he was important, that he was contacted and liked.

"It's HATRAF," Colin said. "They've been trying to connect with you all morning. Me too. I've just been ignoring it..."

"Shit," Ronnie said. He said it like it was any other word in his vocabulary, without inflection or conviction.

He picked up the Screen and tapped to connect back with RAG54. The bot popped up in the room. He swiveled around to take it all in. Ronnie stood by the table, arms limp at his sides. Colin sat on the floor, cross-legged, RIFF23 rolled back and forth behind Ronnie, playing the frowny face emoji. "Ronnie. Colin. Robot," he said.

"I have a name," RIFF23 said.

"I'm sure you do." He heaved a sigh. It was much longer than a human sigh and sounded like the hiss of air released from a tire. "Ronnie, did you not receive my messages?"

"Messages?"

"Messages. Yes."

"No."

"You read them."

"No."

"Ronnie, I can see that you read them. You know that I can see that you read them."

"Maybe I did. I'm sorry. Did I miss something?"

"Yes. Our meeting at 9:00 a.m. today."

"I'm sorry," Ronnie said. He looked around the room as if half-heartedly searching for an explanation, then sat down on the couch.

"Ronnie, I'm just going to cut right to it: You're fired."

"Fired? For one missed meeting?"

"No. You are fired for not doing your job."

"How do you know if I'm doing my job?"

"You filled out some paperwork when you were hired, right?"

"I guess."

"He guesses."

"We've had enough of your attitude!" RIFF23 chimed in.

"Leave it RIFF23," Ronnie advised.

"He guesses."

"We heard you the first time!" RIFF23 rolled through the projection of RAG54, playing a GIF of a punching fist.

"RIFF23, why don't you go outside and cool off?" Ronnie suggested.

"Look, Ron."

"Don't call me that."

"Listen, pal."

"That either."

"Here's the deal. At some point during this hiring process, you were informed that HATRAF is a governmental organization, correct?"

"I guess... Yes."

"You ever hear any rumors about governmental organizations?"

Ronnie shrugged.

"Ask your weirdo friend here. I'm sure he'll tell you some."

Ronnie looked at Colin who rolled his eyes and crossed his arms.

"One such rumor is that we like to spy. I feel I can tell you without the risk of getting in to too much trouble with the big guys that this rumor is true. Most people accept that by now. We had Snowden and Wikileaks, et cetera. You get it, right? I mean humans supposedly get it, but they keep acting in the same dumbass way, so I'm not sure how much they really get it, but supposedly, theoretically you understand the concept.

"Point being, when you are hired by a government agency, when you are some nobody hippie librarian dating some crazy OTG Tech-heiress, working with a drug-fiend who thinks he knows state secrets, your governmental agency of employment is not going to just let you be and hope for the best."

"So you're saying you spied on us," Colin finally spoke up.

"Yes, Bob Dylan. And unless running off to a barely not off-limits zone and getting wasted together is some deep form of rehabilitation, Ronnie is not performing his job duties as prescribed. In fact it would appear Ronnie isn't doing much of anything but living in denial of the fact that he's been dumped."

"The hell you say?" RIFF23 came rumbling through the front door.

"That's all," RAG54 said. "See you never."

He disappeared.

"So, Colin," Ronnie said.

"Yes?"

"Maybe you could explain some of the words used in RAG54's description of you? Such as, I don't know, 'drug fiend' and 'state secrets.'"

"You never made me fill out the intake forms."

"That seems a little beside the point."

"Well on page one of the intake form you would have filled out information about me like name, D.O.B., last employer..."

"Why the hell do you know so much about the intake form?"

"Because of my former employer."

Ronnie stared at him, opened his mouth a little, spread his arms out.

"We're waiting," RIFF23 said, his Screen showing a ticking clock.

"HATRAF," Colin said.

"HATRAF what?"

"HATRAF. That's the answer to the questions you didn't ask me. HATRAF is my former employer."

It went something like this: Colin was a Human/Robot Resources Professional. Ronnie laughed at this while RIFF23 emitted a high-pitch, laugh-like sound. Colin told them they could yuck it up all they wanted, but it was true.

"Are you SHRRM-certified?" RIFF23 asked in mock politeness.

As a matter of fact, he was. He worked in a small department called Preventative HRR. The purpose of Preventative HRR was to monitor employee interaction for red flags. The Pre HRR department spent their hours reading and watching recorded communication among HATRAF's employees, and documenting verbal and non-verbal signs that a disagreement might soon take place. Each time such a pre-disagreement occurred, the guilty parties would be sent to the counselor (humans) or coder (robots) to get some work done. The counselor prescribed mood-stabilizing medications to match whatever issues PHRR perceived. The coder tweaked various personality traits to encourage cooperation.

The problem with Colin was that even though he was SHRRM-certified—even served on the local chapter's board for a while—and excellent at flagging down potential problematic relationships, something about his communication style didn't sit well with people or robots. Even members of the PHRR department had to have their communication monitored, and

Colin's got flagged constantly. At first, his use of exclamation points was seen as too aggressive, so the counselor prescribed sedatives. He seemed too remote, socially cold, so he was given uppers. He mentioned being worried and was prescribed anti-anxiety medication. When he sent a message to a colleague joking about the fact that he couldn't keep all his pills straight, the counselor called him in and offered a time-release capsule that combined all the chemicals in one easy-to-swallow package.

One day—probably right after a release of the capsule—since he felt extremely sleepy but his heart was racing, Colin intercepted a conversation between Field and RAP12, a human and a Robots are Political model respectively who served as co-presidents of HATRAF. The two normally lived up to the expectations of the organization they ran, almost creepily friendly to each other, but something was off this time.

RAP12 asked Field if he was really not going to do anything about HDT. Field responded with an eye-rolling emoji. RAP12 sent five or six angry faces. This was serious, he reminded Field. No, Field assured him. It wasn't serious and he needed to calm down. VS had it under control. *Besides,* Field pointed out, they shouldn't talk about it through work communication channels.

Colin put in a dispute report, citing conflict signs such as negative emoji use and telling a co-worker to be calm.

A week later the counselor called him in. She gave him a pill and a glass of water. After he swallowed, she said, "Your position has been eliminated."

"Just mine?" he asked.

She told him she couldn't discuss such matters. When he went back to his office, everyone else seemed to be going about business as usual. No one looked like they were eliminated. "Anyone got an appointment with the counselor today?" he asked. Most of them ignored him. A few looked up and shook their heads lazily before returning to their Screens.

He went to his cubicle and packed up a box with his succulent and essential oil diffuser. All the Screens in the office started making various beeping and tinkling sounds. His human co-workers glanced at him out of the corners of their eyes. The Robots rolled into a corner and hissed through their speakers.

"I need to go to the bathroom," he said loudly, to no one in particular, and started walking quickly down the hall.

The server room was just past the bathroom. He scanned his badge. It wasn't de-activated yet. Inside he scrambled to the first terminal and tried the administrative password a member of the IT staff gave him when he was too lazy to help him with an install problem: ABC123. He ran a series of searches for the letters "HDT" and quickly slid a chip against the back of the terminal. He loaded hundreds of files onto the chip before he heard ominous clacks and whirring noises coming down the hall. He thought about swallowing the chip but decided instead to stick it in the clump of curls toward the back of his head that hadn't been brushed in a week.

"Colin?" he heard the annoyingly calm voice of the counselor. She knocked lightly on the door. "What are you doing in there?"

When he exited, she stood flanked by three bots. "I got lost," he said lamely.

"Listen, Colin," she said in a falsely sweet tone, "I really hate to do this, but we're gonna have to walk you out."

Back at his apartment, he started going through the files and popping his time-release medication. Figuring out HDT was like reading a letter that was torn in pieces and thrown to you bit by bit, in no particular order.

The first document he opened was a memo.

Memorandum
TO: Executive Staff
FROM: Field Harris
SUBJECT: HDT

It has come to my attention that there has been interdepartmental chatter wrt HDT and the seriousness or perceived lack of seriousness with which I am treating the issue. Let it be known that I am fully aware of the threat posed by such a group and am closely monitoring the situation. I assure the robot contingent of our staff that I take this issue to heart just as if it were threatening my own kind.

Stating such, I ask that the topic not be discussed through departmental communication channels for the time being until the issue of how best to enlighten all HATRAF staff has been settled.

There were aerial photographs of a lake crowded by trees. There were PHRR reports similar to the one Colin filed–co-workers squabbling, throwing the letters HDT around. Then he found the initial report. It was a message sent from an intern in the PR department to the executive in charge of communications.

Sir,
I wanted to make you aware of a potential flash point that I discovered. In my browsing I found reports of a new fringe group–anti-Tech naturalists living near a body of water known as Walden Pond. The body is actually a lake. The group has yet to make any political moves that I can discover, but are slowly gaining membership. They call themselves HDT, an acronym for the name Henry David Thoreau. Thoreau was a 19c transcendentalist who lived along this body of water for a period of time and wrote about it.

The potential for conflict resulting from this group will, like with all these little orgs, depend on how large a following they end up garnering. The reasons for concern that I currently see are the language of the group's founder, a woman named Losi West, who encourages "unplugging" and "freedom."

Find attached some related documents and images.

Colin lost track of how many pills he took. The time release hit him in waves. He was hyper and sleepy and anxious and calm. He scrolled and tapped through the night, forgetting any version of his life that came before, becoming only a brain with fingers. At some point, before the sun rose, Colin closed the last document on the topic of HDT. He didn't remember much that happened next. The police report stated that he showed up at Field's house "yelling obscenities," grabbed a candle, and started to set the house on fire. No one was injured and the fire was quickly doused.

"Did you get arrested?" Ronnie asked.

"Nah, they just threw me in this stupid program."

"Why on earth would they do that?"

Colin shrugged. "I said I'd be quiet. They don't want it in the news. A disgruntled HATRAF employee, not good for the whole goal of kumbaya."

Colin was a defensive sleeper. When Ronnie shook him awake he slapped him in the face and tried to head butt him. Ronnie wrestled him, sat on his stomach and waved a piece of paper in his face.

"The letter!" Ronnie yelled.

Colin blinked up at him. "Ronnie?"

"It's right here in the letter!"

"Lights!"

The lights came on and Colin was confronted with Hil's letter. Ronnie read it out loud to him.

"Yeah, man. You showed it to me already."

"No. Look." He pointed to the letter as he read.

Ronnie,

*It's **Hil**. I'm OK. **Don't** try to find me. I've decided to move on. I trashed the place. I'm trashing my old life. I don't want to see you anymore.*

"Certain letters... It looks like she held the pen down harder. They look bolder. You see it right? It's not just me."

Colin rubbed his eyes and pulled the letter from Ronnie's hand. "Get off me, man."

Ronnie slid down to the floor.

Colin snorted. "HDT," he said.

"They have her?" Ronnie asked.

"It's possible."

"Tell me everything you know."

EIGHT

A woman named Losi West founded the group. She was 5' 2", 95 pounds, with a shaved head, pierced septum, and volatile personality. Losi's parents ran a clean mom and pop brothel for years with many happy politicians and police officers as their customers. The operation was technically illegal, but only in a cute, antiquated way-like how you couldn't tie a camel to a lamppost or keep an ice cream cone in your pocket in some cities. It was an irrelevant law, and no one bothered to try to take it off the books. Mom and Pop Sex Shop was so unscandalous that tagging it as a current location, posting about the great level of service, or sharing a photo of a favorite worker were common practices. When Colin uncovered the HDT investigative files, there were thousands of linked posts about MAPSS featuring everyone from schoolteachers and librarians to mayors and pop stars.

One day, seemingly out of the blue, MAPSS got shut down. The case files were less diffusive on the why of this topic. From the descriptions Colin found, it appeared that many of the wealthy, influential, political-type clients turned against MAPSS. They decided the rules against the existence of such an establishment weren't so antiquated after all, and they fought to have it closed. Colin searched for secondary sources to fill in the gaps. While it was difficult to find anything substantial, the running theory was that lobbyists from VS pressured the local government officials, from the police up to the mayor, to close the business. Colin even found some sites that supposedly had statistics on how badly VS sales were in that area. There were blurry photos of the police chief shaking hands with someone who was supposedly a VS CEO.

Regardless of why or how it came about, the Wests were treated in the typical way of unimportant people who get in the way of important ones–they were made an example. Their hysterical reaction to the verdict–falling on the ground, sobbing–and their dazed-looking daughter being taken down the courthouse steps by a social worker, were all filmed and linked to Losi's file. Colin watched the footage of little Losi West over and over again: the social worker angry and determined, elbowing her way through the gawkers and journalists into a waiting car, Losi in her arms with no expression, her eyes blank and wide, her mouth set, her tight curls bouncing as they moved down the steps.

Rita and Louis immediately adopted Losi. They were in their late 60s and had been in a committed relationship for 30 years. They never had any interest in children, content with their fat cat Alabaster, who hated them and nearly caused the death of each at least once, and a lifestyle that allowed for travel to church retreats and Mahjong tournaments. But when the reverend of their church submitted a plea for someone, anyone, to take Poor Losi and rehabilitate her from a life surrounded by sexual sin, and when he added that the church would offer an annual stipend plus life-long Tech for the child and whoever took her in, they decided that, heck, it might be worth a shot. The official report on Losi was less colorful on the details, simply stating the names of her adoptive parents.

The records HATRAF obtained from her bot, RIFF512, gave a more personalized image of Losi's new parents. In fact, after her adoption, the government trail died down significantly, beyond the general cloud of knowledge about her search habits and interests (Punk Rock, Her Parents, Unfair Imprisonment, Loneliness) and Colin depended on RIFF512's records to find out what happened next. When Losi once again became a subject of interest to the States government, her bot was taken into custody and questioned. Colin pulled up the audio file of one of the interviews and played it for Ronnie and RIFF23.

DEPOSITION BY COMPANION BOT RIFF512 WRT RECENT ACTIVITIES PERPETRATED BY LOSI WEST

What can I say about Losi? I hated her. It might not have been her fault, and yet it definitely was her fault. What I mean is she may have been a perfectly nice person not deserving to be hated, but she programmed me to hate her so there was nothing I could do about it. There's debate in the AI community regarding whether or not pure emotions like love and hate can actually be experienced by bots. When one of Losi's adopted parents says, muffled behind a closed bedroom door, that she hates Losi, and when I say I hate Losi, are we experiencing the same thing? Do my programmed clipped answers, desire to move into a different room, and the confusion in my coding that make me unable to communicate with her match some sort of blood-pressure-rising, straight-set-mouth, heart-pounding feeling? I can't say, really. I am wires and buttons and humans are a whole bunch of gross things mashed up together.

Whatever it was I felt, the human emotion it seems most similar to is hate. It wasn't always that way, but we never had a typical relationship. When I was first presented to her by her new parents, I didn't like or dislike Losi. I didn't have a personality or anything. I just responded to what she said and roamed around the house. Little Losi would turn me off a lot, so I missed huge chunks of her development. She never confided in me or anything, but I think it's safe to say she was a pretty angry person. Her parents basically never talked to her, and left her alone for weeks at a time to go on trips. She spent a lot of her time researching her parents, zooming in on their images, reading article after article about their case. Most people agreed their imprisonment was completely unjust, but there were some who were glad to see "those perverts" punished. Losi didn't discriminate and she didn't filter. She read it all: the good and the bad. She read in-depth think pieces on the case, she read entire books that just mentioned her parents in one sentence as an example. If her parents' names were somewhere, she found them and she read. This was the only contact she had with the Wests. Her new parents didn't allow her to receive any of their messages, to message them back, and certainly not to visit them. She never participated in any way in the discussion revolving around her parents–not so much as a like or a comment–even when there were specific allusions to her person, and there were quite a few. Everyone wanted to know what happened to that stunned little girl they'd seen on the courtroom steps. Besides reading about her parents all the time, what Losi did was go to school. She never brought any friends home or communicated with them via Tech. As she got older, she started to listen to punk music. She mostly liked this person called Iggy Pop. She watched hours of video of him throwing up, bleeding, and screaming. Like everything else in her life, she participated in this hobby alone. She never commented, shared, or liked anything.

As she got older, she started tinkering with me more. She made me like her. Not "like her" like her, but **like** her, as in, similar to her. She was quiet, she was anti-social, she was angry. So was I. I often wondered if our relationship was similar to that of other humans and companions. I knew that there were companion groups that met up and discussed things, supported each other, bitched, whatever, but it was not in me to go to such a meeting. My automatic response to the idea was disgust: "Only a bunch of idiots would want to sit around and share their feelings."

When she was a kid she had these unruly curls that she hid behind. She had big, brown eyes and a straight-set mouth. She was small for her age—both short and thin—the clothes her adopted parents bought her would hang limply from her bony frame. As she got older, her features grew more pronounced. She stayed thin and short but she was given an allowance for clothes that she used to buy fitted black outfits and thick boots. When she turned 16 she shaved her head and pierced her septum. Her adopted parents never commented on the change. I know about Western beauty standards and I've seen plenty of models and actresses. Losi was very beautiful. But as far as I could tell, she never went on a date, never was invited to a dance, she never even received messages from other kids her age, unless it was something minor and boring like clarification on a homework assignment. Even these seemed to be sent with extreme hesitancy, as if they were afraid of her, always profusely apologizing for bothering her and then thanking her way too much for whatever small, often unhelpful, response she gave.

Her voice was deep and raspy. She spoke so infrequently, not just to me, but at all, that I was startled whenever I heard her voice. Whenever she did speak, almost always to ask me what time it was, it took me a moment to add it up, to realize that it was Losi speaking, that the voice was coming from her tiny body, that she could speak, that she was talking to me, that she was saying: "Hello? Did you hear me? What time is it?"

Now that I've been reprogrammed to what is considered a normal behavioral level, I think I understand Losi better. I don't think she wanted me to. She made me cut off—gave me no empathy for her, no interest in what she was feeling. I was angry with her and I didn't know why. That was what she wanted. She didn't want to care about me and she didn't want me to care about her. I don't know if she wanted me to feel how she suffered—because that's how it feels, to be that angry, that alone, it hurts, it is a way of suffering—or if she just wanted to be left alone, to hide in her anger.

She finally managed to separate herself from me for good. There was some punk band she was following. I can't remember what they were called exactly. The Merry Christmases or The Happy Chanukahs or something weird like that. She listened to them all the time and obsessively read this community page where other fans discussed them. Of course, she never posted or liked anything, just read. When she was reading the discussions she actually made a variety of facial expressions, which was rare. I would look over and see her smiling, even chuckling to herself. Sometimes she would listen to their music and cry quietly. One day the band announced that they would be playing in a town nearby. Losi decided she was going. This was strange in itself, because Losi never went anywhere. Even stranger was the fact that Losi commented on their post: "Be there!" using smiley face emojis with heart eyes and lots of exclamation points. The post was made about a week before the concert, and she walked around smiling that whole week. She even said hi to me a few times when our paths crossed, and was much more polite when she asked me what time it was.

And then, well, that was the end, I guess. She left for the concert in the CAR provided by the church, which she had never ridden in before. When she came back she marched in the house, coming straight toward me. I remember thinking, as she walked toward me, that maybe she was going to reprogram me. I remember wondering if she was going to say something nice to me, because she *looked happy and she looked determined and she was walking right at me. I remember hoping, because it was hard. I felt strained. Being angry and hateful all the time is hard on a robot. My coding felt all tied up and confused. My wires felt like they would get fried at any time. I felt exhausted and like my programs weren't working the way they were supposed to. I hoped she would change me. Fix me. I remember thinking, "Please fix me."*

That's the last thing I remember. Then I woke up and I was here, with you people. She had turned me off, I guess.

#

"So... What happened?" Ronnie asked.

"No one knows, exactly," Colin said. "She went to a concert like RIFF512 said. The band was actually called Kill Santa. No one at the show would confirm that they saw her. I guess all those punks stick together. But there were cams that show her there. They even show her talking to people, dancing around, smiling. But I guess what's important is what happened after she left the show. Her CAR recorded an hour-long pit stop at Walden Pond.

"I'm really not sure why she turned RIFF512 off, like she might as well have just left her there to live her bot days alone with the adoptive parents, because she went back to Walden a few days later. There were all these Tent People who lived in the woods around Walden. The theory is Losi recruited them and they built a sort of community.

"The thing I can't figure out is why all this was allowed to go on. The land around Walden was all abandoned, sure, so there weren't any landowners complaining or anything, but the authorities didn't do anything about it. It's like they thought she was just too much of a nuisance to bother with, and they let her be. But her group just started growing.

"Oh and, one other thing she did, after she turned off RIFF512 and before she returned to Walden, she made this video."

He pulled it up. On his Screen sat shave-headed Losi. She was in a bedroom that must have been hers, but seemed at odds with her person: pink floral bedspread, satin curtains, and beige carpet. She wore shorts and a t-shirt, hugged a pillow, and looked away from the camera. She talked about Henry David Thoreau, about Walden. The fact that Losi never had any friends and rarely talked was apparent in the video. She looked nervous. She kept twisting the corner of the pillow in her hands. A blush crept from her neck to her scalp. When she was done with her speech she made a nervous sound with her throat before the video cut out.

"That was a couple of years ago," Colin said.

"They have Hil," Ronnie said.

He flipped furiously through photos Colin pulled up of HDT–surveillance footage of masked young people sneaking into houses and planting bombs outside of Tech companies. He looked for Hil, hoping he'd see her slender wrists sticking out from a black shirt, a familiar green in the eyes above a bandana-covered face. He did not see her. If he saw her, he did not know her.

NINE

The end of my relationship with Johns sent me into a depression that verged on panic. It was an odd sort of mental breakdown; because in the self-assured part of my brain, tucked behind my right eyebrow, I had a little message playing on repeat telling me that I didn't really need him. He'd been my on-again off-again sidekick since Nature School, an expected presence. At times I wasn't even sure I actually liked him at all or if I was just used to having him around. Everyone called him my boyfriend and me his girlfriend, but it was never anything we'd agreed upon, just something comfortable we slipped into. When he said he wanted to break up I just blinked at him for a while, then I said, calmly, because I wasn't feeling much, "Do we even go out?" He took this as some sort of bitchy, faux-laid-back statement, and stormed off. For a few days I didn't think much about the situation or Johns. We'd often go days without communicating. He refused to do VV or PO or any of my old-fashioned shit, and he had to go on trips with his family a lot, so there was plenty of dead time between F2Fs. About three days after the breakup I felt like seeing him. So I showed up at his house per usual, but when he came to the door he seemed unhappy to see me and then this girl came to the door behind him, all gorgeous and tall and with big boobs, and he said, "I can't really hang out right now, Hil," and then I understood. It was like when the dentist sprays your teeth with that high-pressure thing and then they stick that vacuum tube in your mouth and–slurp–it's all gone. The part of my life that involved Johns–the hours of listening to his idiotic politics, him rolling his eyes at my Tech refusals, nights not thinking about those things, just getting wasted and laughing, that was all sucked up leaving me clean and dry.

So Georgie invited me to a party and I decked myself out like a Christmas present and put on my blue mascara that makes my eyes look insane and I went. When I got there, Johns was with some different beautiful, tall, big-boobed individual and we exchanged pleasantries and it was all pretty OK. I didn't feel much toward him, just sort of a loneliness that flew out from me and looked for somewhere to perch. I felt him looking at me throughout the evening, but I avoided looking back. I guess I was waiting to see what would happen.

Something happened when I saw Ronnie, in that moment, before he was a formed human with all his annoying parts and endearing parts. He was tall and lithe, with bright eyes, and slender, clean hands. When he left me to go find his bot, I stood, swaying slowly to the music, waiting. Johns jerking my arm interrupted my daydream.

"What the hell?" I yelled as he dragged me into a corner. "Get off of me!" I shoved him against a wall and started toward the hallway where I saw Ronnie returning.

He grabbed me again, held me by the wrist, and said in a soft, pleading voice, "Hil, we need to talk."

"Fuck off, sir," I replied in my best Secret Service voice.

"Hil. Stop. Look. OK. You were right."

"About what?"

"About everything. I know I should have listened before. I was just, I don't know, it was like I knew you too well to take you seriously."

"Whatever that means."

"I know it sounds stupid, but it's the only way I can figure it. But now I know. And I'm sorry."

"Sorry. I missed something. What do you know?"

"About Walden."

"So... what? You're saying you stole one of my books? Well, I'm glad you can actually read. I was never sure."

"I deserve that. But seriously, I read Losi's manifesto. I know about Walden. I realize now that you were right."

"Who the fuck is Losi?"

"You haven't seen this Dark Web stuff?"

I stared at him, nonplussed.

"Well... right... I mean... of course you haven't, but I just thought... I don't know. It's so much you that I just thought you must have something to do with it."

"I still don't know what you're talking about."

"I know. Look, this isn't a good place... Can we go for a walk?"

I looked around the corner and saw Ronnie and his bot. I sighed. Johns was feeling persistent and I would not be able to get rid of him.

"Alright. Fine."

"Thank you. I like your sweater, by the way."

"Shut up."

We did circles around Georgie's block and Johns told me about Losi and Walden. He told me he was going to go join Losi, to further her cause.

"What do you mean by 'further'?" I asked, remembering Johns' tendency to take good ideas and turn them into bad ideas.

"I mean take action. Act. Do the things her ideas support."

"Sounds like her idea is basically 'live in the woods,' so all you really need to do is that."

"Come on, Hil, this is so in your wheelhouse. Tech has taken over everything. This is a chance to find some like-minded people and do something about it."

We walked for a while, silently, coming around the corner again just in time to see Ronnie get into a CAR.

"I'm just wondering when you became 'like-minded'," I said, finally.

"What do you mean?"

"I mean all the years I've known you, you called my anti-Tech talk paranoia. You refused to PO or VV. And now we break up and all the sudden I'm right?"

"I know. I was a dick. But after we... When I started seeing new people... I mean you've been in my life practically all my life, you know? When you were around we all put that stuff up, and I guess that became routine, so that even when you and I weren't hanging out anymore, I just didn't really feel the need to pull my Screen out. But then, you know, I start seeing some new girls and it's like, it's constant. I think I never realized what a big problem it was, because I was so used to you and our friends and, thanks to you, we kept all of that at a low level. Now I start introducing these new people to my life and they drive me crazy and it makes me depressed. I'll be having a nice conversation with a woman, thinking we're really hitting it off, and then I realize she's making a video, taking a picture, even just in an open meeting and letting her friends hear what I'm saying. It's fucking creepy."

"But it's been like this for forever."

"That's what I always say, and you say it comes in waves, and I want to lead a new wave."

"OK."

"OK? You'll come?"

"Come? No. Why do I need to have anything to do with this? I already changed."

"But you could lead others."

"No thanks."

"Hil, how can you not care?"

"I do care, that's why I try to influence people like you to do better. But I've tried the whole mass influence thing with the ZTs and people just end up thinking you're someone you're not. There's this whole persona business I really don't like, and like, I don't know, they can say three things about you that are 100% true, but something about the way the facts are stated, or purposely combined or something, it turns them into a lie."

Johns asked me to think about it. I told him I would, but I didn't really plan on it. That night, after watching some boring 90s rom-com about a guy who calls in to a radio show with my mom, I found I couldn't stop. It was this Losi person. Something about her, about the bits of her manifesto Johns told me, this picture I had of her alone on Walden with the wildflowers; it made me sort of sad and curious. I decided to go to the studio and do some research. RIFF3131 was very excited when I arrived. She loved research and had been bored all week.

We found Losi's post. She looked small and scared–head shaved, arms hugging her pink pillow, combat boots unlaced. Her low, melodic voice was at odds with her image.

"There are things I've been thinking about lately," she started out, then sighed. "I think about my parents always, of course, and the people who took them away from me and how it was all for nothing. It was all for a thousandth of a percent loss of profit.

"Henry David Thoreau once wrote: 'so thoroughly and sincerely are we compelled to live, reverencing our life, and denying the possibility of change. This is the only way, we say, but there are as many ways as there can be drawn radii from one centre.' And when I read that it was like I wrote it because I knew it to be true. What do we do? What do we do? We do nothing. We sit and look for things to entertain us. We walk around in the world and document our walking around and check to see what other are saying about our walking around. There's no break from it, there is no real or actual, even if I put an apple in front of you that is fresh from a tree and you can touch it and it is in your presence, there is still no real or actual apple because you are thinking: 'what is it that I read about the health benefits of apples?' or 'Retta likes apples, I'll take a picture and send it to her,' or 'I should message everyone and tell them that I ate this apple.' So we take what is real and we turn it unreal. But at Walden it is not like this. At Walden, I cannot tell you really, because the telling is what causes the unrealness. What I want to say is just go there if you wish. It is where I will be. No Screens and no bots, of course. Come and live and be real."

"Sounds like a hippie," RIFF3131 said.
"You think everyone's a hippie."
"True."
"I'm going to write her a letter."
"Of course you are."
And I did. I supplemented the things Johns had told me with my own research. In the letter I told her I was sorry about

her parents and that I had the same basic beliefs when it came to the separation we had from reality. I also sent her a book about the last OTG movement, which was eventually ruined by some corporate asshole who decided to bring back retro Tech and everyone started carrying beepers and wearing calculator watches and within a year we were back to Screens.

By the time Losi wrote me back, Johns had disappeared and I'd started seeing Ronnie. It all bled together into one confusing swirl. I wanted to swallow him up, to memorize him, to blink and know all there was to know about him from birth to death. So we became a couple in a way that Johns and I never were–a unit–entwined and messy.

Dear Hil,

Johns has told me so much about you. You are an inspiration. Thank you for your book and your words. I hope to repay your kindness a little with this stationary. It reminds me of what Walden once was, and fills me with a sort of calm. Please write to me more. Tell me about your life. And consider joining us.

XO

Losi

Included in the package with her letter were small, white cards and envelopes printed with big green lily pads. Walden was actually a lake and likely never had lily pads, but I appreciated the gesture. I wrote back. I told her a little about Ronnie. I declined her invitation to join HDT. She kept writing and asking me to join, I kept writing back and saying no. She told me about what it was like there, I told her what was going on in my life.

Shit started to get weird. Losi wrote to me a more urgent request to join HDT, saying she felt her voice was getting lost in the group, that she felt like only I understood her and her intentions. She said she started out angry, but Walden brought her peace, and now all she saw from Johns and the rest of the group was an anger that could not be calmed. I declined her invitation again. I told her I was sorry, that I understood her frustrations, and that I knew how Johns was. He could quickly become the only voice anyone heard. It was people like him who stopped me from joining organizations, who caused me to stop attending meetings for groups who supported causes about which I was passionate. "I've always found it better to work on my own," I ended the letter. "Maybe that's what's best for you too."

Then Johns showed up with his dirty hippie buddies. He even got someone to handwrite me a letter, asked in his sweetest Johns way if I'd meet him. He wanted to catch up. I wrote back: "Warehouse. Friday. Two." I had a date with Ronnie that night that I didn't want to cancel, and I didn't want to have to tell him about this–letter writing a cult leader, rendezvous with exes. Up to that point, we had no secrets, but this seemed like too much to share. I was hoping I could just take care of it all. End it with Johns. Tell him to leave me alone once and for all.

#

Johns started going to The Warehouse because he was a bored, rich, asshole teenager. Nowhere appealed more to bored, rich, asshole teenagers than The Outskirts-full of people who weren't bored or rich and only some of whom were assholes. I've dealt with the impulse my whole life, so I won't judge Johns too harshly on it, but there's something about privilege that breeds a patronizing obsession with the unprivileged. All Johns wanted to do was hang out with people who weren't like him, preferably ones who were mixed up in some fucked up shit.

"I met X the other day. Dude's mixed up in some fucked up shit," he'd say to me every few months. Then Johns would go along with X through his fucked up shit—running around, dodging Y, paying off Z, threatening W, until things got to a level where Johns was scared. And that's all it was after all, a way to escape reality with the wild-eyed conspiracy theorists, the tired sex workers, and the drugged-out 90s freaks.

I can't say for sure if my intentions in going to The Warehouse were completely pure, but I'd like to think so. I listened to Johns brag about his visits there with never more than an eye roll for acknowledgement. Then Chele had her Experience.

Sweet Chele. She had these beautiful straight white teeth that she flashed for no reason, a soft mumbling way of speaking, so you had to lean in close to hear, and atrocious fashion sense. She had a thing for floral, but not in a cool vintage or ironic way.

Chele, age 16, woke up to the old cliché: a flashing light, feeling paralyzed, a prolonged period of semi consciousness, followed by waking up days later in a field far from her house with a little v-shaped scar next to her armpit.

"She always wore those floral prints," people started to say, implying she'd just been crazy all along.

"They're here," Chele told me, holding my hand in the hospital.

"Who?" I asked.

"VS"

"VS?"

"Very scary."

I felt it was insensitive at the time to ask her why she'd started speaking in abbreviations.

"Who's very scary?" I asked.

"I don't know who they are," she said, her voice weak and cracking, frustrated, "I just know that they're here."

"You should take her to The Warehouse," Johns suggested, and when I finished rolling my eyes I realized it was a good idea.

We were young then–all hopes, dreams, and hormones. Chele, sweet and timid, was afraid of The Warehouse, didn't want to go alone, so I came along, swimming laps in the pool while she joined The Believers. I sunk to the bottom of the pool, floated above the moon painted there. I took in the tower and the craters and the shadows and as I held my breath I thought about Chele—about what happened to her and how she felt afraid and powerless—and about Johns—how sometimes he was so selfish and demanding that it felt like peace, like the bottom of the pool to be without him. I looked at the moon and I remembered what Chele said: "They're here."

I never went back to The Warehouse after that. Chele felt safe after the first meeting and seemed to prefer to go alone.

When I entered The Warehouse, the girl at the door told me that Johns was waiting for me in The Coffee Shop. Distracted by the pictures lining the walls, I bumped into someone coming the other way. We both let out a surprised chirp then stood and looked at each other for a moment. When I looked at her, I thought about the craters on the moon, maybe because of the scar on her face, though it was a raised v and not a crater. She was me was the thing. Well, she wasn't me, because I was me, but she was me-like: her hair the same uninteresting brown, her eyes and nose and mouth all different shapes from mine, but something about the way they were combined reminded me of me, of how I felt or how I felt I looked. We were about the same height and she wore an outfit I would wear: jeans too tight, shirt too big around the shoulders, sandals pinching her toes, nail polished chipped, eyeliner smeared. I could sense in her, in her me-like face that she had the same thoughts, but we also shared the thought that we would say nothing, so we smiled shyly and continued on our way.

The barista at The Coffee Shop had dirty Kurt Cobain hair and a hostile approach to his work.

"Ju want?" he asked, wiping down the counter and avoiding eye contact.

I ordered a small coffee, black, which caused him to roll his eyes for some reason before thrusting a stained mug at me, the contents sloshing over the rim and burning my fingers. I winced, issued a pathetically passive "thank you," and went to join Johns, who waited like a noir character in a dark corner, a dumb-looking brimmed hat shading his eyes, both hands wrapped around an inappropriately unserious whipped-cream-topped beverage. I slid into the seat across from him, wiping my wet hands on my skirt.

"You look pissed as usual," was the first thing he said.

"This is my face," I responded, already feeling exhausted by him, "you've known me my whole life. You know this."

"Still a pretty face."

"Please shut up and get on with it."

He grinned at me. I tried, and failed, to keep myself from grinning back.

"Losi needs you," he said after a few seconds of silent sipping.

"No. She wants me. If she needed me she would say so. She's not the type to send a goon after me to bust my balls."

"Goon? Balls? This is sounding very Scorsese all of a sudden."

"Since when do you know about Scorsese?" I grew more annoyed. I'd never been able to get Johns to watch a movie with me.

"I know things," he said with a shrug.

"What the fuck do you want, Johns? You're acting like a creep."

"I want you to come to Walden," he said.

"Oh. Ok. Well. No," I said, getting up to leave.

He didn't move. I turned and walked out of The Coffee Shop, looking back once to see him take a sip of his drink, lifting his head with a whipped cream mustache. The barista glared at me and I smiled and flipped him off. Further down the hallway, I heard water splashing and voices echoing, I remembered the pool and decided to check it out. Most of the women sitting around the pool were thin and beautiful, most of the men were buff and scary. I reached out to grab a cucumber sandwich from a passing RAS, then looked up to see a lily pad painted on the ceiling of the pool room. It looked identical to the one on the cards Losi sent me. My chest felt tight. I turned to leave, bumping into coffee shop Kurt Cobain.

"Where ya headed?" he asked, grinning at me maliciously.

"Home," I replied as I tried to push my way past him to the door.

"Cool." He grabbed my shoulders as I attempted to circumnavigate his flannel-clad body. "I can give you a ride."

"I'm good. Thanks," I began to feel scared, and tried shrugging him off.

"No. I don't think you are good, bitch," he said, grabbing my arms, pinning them behind my back, and pushing me out the door.

I yelled for help, but no one even looked in our direction. Outside, Johns waited in the backseat of a CAR. Kurt shoved me and got into the driver's seat. A guy with dreadlocks piled on top of his head, a scraggly beard, and dirty fingernails sat in the passenger-side seat.

"What the fuck is this about, Johns?" I yelled in his face.

He smiled calmly and shrugged. "You know what it's about."

"HDT? You had Smells Like Teen Spirit break my arm so I'll come hang with you in the woods?"

"It's much more than that, Hil, and you know it."

"I know that you are crazy. I do know that. And what exactly do you plan to do now? Kidnap me?"

"You're an adult," the gross guy with dreads chimed in.

"Adult nap!" Kurt Cobain chuckled. I kicked his seat.

"Chill, Hil," Johns said. "We're just taking you home. I wanted a little more time to talk to you to see if I could get you to change your mind."

We pulled up outside of the studio and Kurt Cobain continued his crime goon act by pulling me out of the car and holding on to me as we entered the building.

"You're seriously going to let him act like this, Johns?" I asked.

Johns shrugged.

# #

"Who are these hippies?" RIFF3131 greeted us at the door.

"Can you like call the police or something?" I asked RIFF3131.

"Well, I'd have to leave a message. It's after hours."

"Let's just sit down for a minute," Johns suggested in a placating tone.

Kurt shoved me onto the couch. Johns sat beside me.

"Hil Hil Hil." Johns said, slowly shaking his head. "You're a fucking traitor, you know that? Look at all of this shit. The girl who invented the Zen Tent has a Screen and a RIFF model."

"Dumbass dumbass dumbass," I replied, "You have been here before so don't act surprised. Also, what do you want?"

"You."

"How romantic."

"Not like that. Well... that would be nice too, but I meant more like 'Uncle Sam Wants You!'... except the opposite of that."

"Johns, you've known me a long time, what about me makes you think that 'no' is something I don't mean?"

"You're right, Hil. I have known you a long time. Your whole life almost. So I know you are annoyingly stubborn and distractingly beautiful."

"God, I wish you would shut up."

"But I also know about the things that matter to you most. I know how to convince you." He took something out of his pocket and began rubbing it between his fingers.

"What do you have?" I asked.

"Wouldn't you like to know?"

"Of course I would like to know, but also since your plan seems to be some sort of blackmail or something I'd assume that you want me to know too."

"That's a good call," dreadlocks said, nodding seriously, his eyes stoned, glazed over.

He opened his hand and held out his palm to display a dime-sized silver star.

I stared at him, slowly shook my head.

"See?" Johns said.

I got up and ran at him. He pushed me and I fell on the floor. RIFF3131 rolled over to me playing an emoji of a fist.

"You were onto something with the whole blackmail thing, Hil," Johns said.

"Give it back," I said, getting up off the floor.

"I'm going to give you a month," he continued, "and if you decide not to help the cause, this" he held up the star, "will happen."

I stared at Johns. All I could say was, "I trusted you."

Johns looked disturbed for a moment, then shook his head. "That was your mistake."

TEN

Colin and Ronnie got jobs. They weren't the kind of jobs people admitted to having. Ronnie preferred to pretend he was unemployed. When he ran into an acquaintance who asked what he was up to, he would say vague things like "I enjoy the city. I go on walks. I often try different restaurants." This earned him raised eyebrows and kind pats on the back.

They were moderators for a mind-numbingly boring Group Hang for ten tween girls. They were responsible for combing through abbreviations and emojis, noting anything inappropriate or out of the ordinary, then sending a report to each person's parent. The pay was depressingly low and there was nothing rewarding about telling Mr. and Mrs. Warren that Thatch was having her period and that was why she cried during dinner.

Colin, RIFF23, and Ronnie spent their free time searching the Dark Web for intel on Hil. Colin went on "recon" to The

Warehouse showing pictures of Hil, and getting no helpful responses. Ronnie read Colin's HDT file over and over again. He even wrote a form letter to his congressman expressing his concerns about Hil, from which he received an automated response thanking him for his "various political interests."

A few weeks after he saw her at The Warehouse, Gret projected in. She was thinner and paler than Ronnie remembered.

He'd given up on seeing her again, after putting in ten requests (all denied) and turning away a substitute. Finally, he tried to file a formal complaint. A message popped up to tell him that "technical difficulties" made this option "temporarily unavailable." That's when she showed up.

"Where have you been?"

"Busy," she said in a monotone, sitting on his bed.

"At The Warehouse?"

"I don't know what you're talking about."

"I saw you..."

"I don't know what you're talking about."

She flickered for a moment then disappeared.

He tried contacting her again. An error message appeared informing him that his account had been deactivated for "inappropriate behavior." He tried contacting reactivation services, but was told that feature was only available to individuals with active accounts.

He went to sleep. He dreamt that he was standing in the middle of dense woods. There was a break in the trees ahead where sunlight came in. He walked toward the light. When he came to the opening in the trees he saw a pond filled with lily pads. The man in the tuxedo from The Believers stood in the middle of the pond. He wore his tuxedo and stared at Ronnie, emitting a high-pitched, horrific scream.

Ronnie heard a rustling in the woods behind him. He turned to see Hil standing on the path. She stood very still with her hands limp at her sides. She looked straight through him. "Hil!" he called. She didn't respond, but turned and walked slowly, deeper into the woods. He ran after her, but as he ran the path grew longer, and she got farther away. It grew dark. He stopped. Hil appeared before him again, this time inches away, her face level with his chest. She had the sleepy, red-eyed look she got when she was trying not to cry. Her mouth twisted to the side. He reached out to stroke her hair, but she disappeared.

He woke to a banging on the door. His heart raced from the dream and he was filled with a deep dread. He heard RIFF23 answer the door and then a familiar female voice. For a moment he thought it was Hil and he was paralyzed with happiness, with relief, but the visitor continued to speak and he realized it was not Hil's voice that he recognized, but a much stranger one: one belonging to someone who should not be knocking on his door. RIFF23 came into his bedroom.

"Ronnie, there's a person here..."

"Gret?"

RIFF23 played a checkmark emoji.

Gret pushed past RIFF23, into Ronnie's room, and stood at the foot of his bed. Ronnie tried to rectify in his mind the idea of real Gret standing where light and sound Gret usually stood. With her close like this, he could further sense the fleshy reality of her existence that he first became aware of at The Warehouse pool. Her hair was greasy, piled on her head in a messy bun. She wore faded black yoga pants and an oversized t-shirt proclaiming: "Daytona Beach." She remained at the foot of his bed, arms crossed, looking impatient, as if he'd invited her there and she was waiting to see what he had to say.

"So this is the real you?" he said finally. Standing up awkwardly, beginning to walk toward her, then stopping at the side of his bed, arms hanging limply.

"I shouldn't be here," she said, pulling at her t-shirt where it slipped down her shoulder.

"Yes. It does seem not normal."

"Well, aren't you wondering why I'm here?"

"Sorry. Did I do something to annoy you?"

"Your lack of curiosity annoys me."

"I'm curious! I just... I'm having a hard time here lately, and I just woke up from a nap."

"I'm here about Hil."

"You have... you know... how do you even know who Hil is?"

She rolled her eyes and crossed her arms even tighter. Ronnie noticed that RIFF23 was still in the doorway, rolling eyes repeating on his Screen.

"RIFF23, can you give us a sec?"

RIFF23 left and the door closed behind him.

"Do you remember when you signed up for VS?"

Ronnie shrugged.

"You had to sign some stuff?"

"There was paperwork. Definitely lots of paperwork."

"Did you read all of this paperwork?"

"Probably not."

"Probably not?"

"Definitely not."

"It's pretty delicate what we have to deal with at VS."

"Sure."

"It takes a lot. It takes knowing a lot."

"OK."

"You think you might have signed away some personal freedoms in all that paperwork?"

"Yeah. Probably."

"OK now that we're done with the little thought experiment, yes, I know about Hil. She's in your file."

"My file?"

"Connect the dots here, Ronnie. You sign away your life to VS, we access your files, we make a little dossier type thing on you, we keep tabs."

"Tabs were kept?"

"Hil goes missing. You come to The Warehouse. People don't like it."

"People?"

"Various interests."

"So that's why you told me to leave?"

"There was some talk once you showed up. People wondering if you were going to cause trouble. My bodyguard was told to watch you closely. Client and service provider interaction outside of the virtual world is not encouraged for one thing, for another your file indicated volatility-causing life circumstances and a desire to stir up shit."

"I don't understand. What sort of shit?"

"There are different groups that like to hang out at The Warehouse. VS is one of those groups. In general all the groups leave each other alone. There are plenty of paranoid individuals walking the halls, though, and VS personnel are on high alert for such individuals. If such an individual, say one with a high volatility rating and a significant other who hates Tech, shows up, they take precautionary measures."

"Like what?"

"It's hard to say."

"I guess it's good I left."

"Yes, I think so too."

They stood facing each other for a few moments. Ronnie contemplated aspects of her that were different from her projected form. She was taller than him. The half-circle of skin beneath her right eye was slightly dark, giving her a tired tinge. She had freckles along the bridge of her nose, and without her rosy-red lipstick her lips were small and thin.

He sighed. "What do you know?"

She sat on the edge of his bed, put her hands flat on her knees and examined her nails. He noticed the slivers of nail that showed at the bottom of each grown out manicure. He sat beside her, looked at her profile, felt the strangeness of smelling her, of seeing her indentation on his mattress.

"It will be hard to tell. You'll have to bear with me. It's not some nice story with a beginning, middle, and end. It's more like... I don't know. It's like a dream. All these random unconnected things passing by, and you'd have to be paranoid to think they have anything to do with one another, to think it's all one big story and all the pieces fit together. I only have some of the pieces. Some of them fit. Some of them don't. Some of them might belong to a different puzzle."

"What do you know about Hil?"

"I have this client. He's not just my client. He uses lots of girls. His name is Johns. He's rich and his dad's high up in the government, director of the NSA or something. I don't work with him much. Not his type I guess. But recently he requested me. It was weird. When I showed up he just stood there and talked at me. He asked me some questions but didn't really listen to my answers.

"Then he asked me if I ever considered that I had a higher calling? Sure, I told him. I thought I'd be a nun one day. He didn't laugh. Just nodded and smiled. Then he asked me if I ever thought I was bringing harm to people, offering my services. I asked if he was upset with me, if I'd brought harm to him. He shook his head, said I was missing the point. Told me there was this group that would show me. 'Show me what?' I asked. He said 'lots of things.' They'd show me my job was the root of the evil in this world, not because of what I did but because of how I did it. Told me that being there in the room with him like that was some sort of abomination."

"A group?"

"They're called HDT."

"How did you..."

"I'll get there. So I peaced out of that situation. I asked around. Some of the other girls got a similar pitch. Supposedly a couple that quit around then were following this guy. I don't know if that's true. I don't know about a lot of what I'm telling you.

"Then a week or so later, right before I saw you at The Warehouse, before Hil disappeared, I got audited. They said they were going to pick one client at random, check the files and make sure I was doing my job right. The client they chose to audit was you.

"It wasn't normal, though, because they told me they were going to 'continuously monitor the situation' and they watched all of our sessions and kept asking for more intel. They'd never done that before and I didn't understand why with you, because you were so normal and I knew I was following all protocols properly.

"So like, VS has permission to read your messages and stuff. We don't normally do that unless we feel we're at risk of losing a client, to try to figure out what's going on in their life that we can play off of, but they wanted a daily rundown of your messages, your check-ins, everything.

"Then Hil disappeared. It was strange being there as it happened, watching your messages go out. They told me that this turn of events might cause future client-professional issues and so I needed to monitor closely and report. I had to provide daily reports on your life and mood.

"When you came to The Warehouse, they took me off your case. They didn't do it officially, as you know, that's why you were still able to request me. I was just told not to show up because you exhibited erratic behavior by stalking me. But since technically you were still my client, I don't know, I was curious. I kept reading your messages. That's when I saw that you were looking into HDT."

Ronnie felt like he should be more excited about new information, but he felt tired. Gret was like an interesting TV show he was watching before bed. He wanted to know what happened, but his consciousness kept nodding in and out.

"My mom loves the Antichrist. I mean, I guess technically she doesn't love him, but she loves to talk about him and worry about him and predict who he will be."

"Or she."

"Or she. Sure. There's this part she loves to quote. 'I considered the horns, and, behold, there came up among them another little horn, before whom there were three of the first horns plucked up by their roots: and, behold, in this horn were eyes like the eyes of men, and a mouth speaking great things."

"What the hell." It was a bland statement. Not a question. He was growing increasingly confused by her story and increasingly sad about Hil, but tried to stick to conversational conventions.

"Yeah! So creepy, right? But, well, I guess that's a little beside the point. I never can really understand what it's supposed to mean, except the 'speaking great things' part, which is what she always emphasizes, probably because none of the other words around it make sense. She takes it to mean that he... or she... will be some very charismatic, persuasive person. I sound crazy, I know, but that is what I thought when I first met Johns. It's not a normal client set up with people like him. The way this guy looks... he is beautiful. Like in a way women are supposed to be. And then when he starts to talk... It's like whatever he says must be true. He will look you in the eyes and tell you things you know are crazy and wrong, but you will nod at him and smile and think maybe you are the one who is crazy and wrong."

"He's a talking horn. Or whatever."

"Or whatever. I feel afraid when I talk to him, but also I feel like I could keep listening to him talk, keep nodding my head, forever. Until I get away from him. That's when I feel truly, just afraid. He gets in my head. And he is always... he just seems so blameless. So good and caring and thoughtful. But he isn't.

"Like, once he requested my friend and when she showed up he told her he was worried about her. She really felt it was true, felt his concern. He said he heard she'd been having a hard time. She broke down. She was having some issues with drugs and a breakup and stuff. She told him everything. He comforted her, told her everything was going to be OK. Told her he was going to help her. He kept requesting her back over and over again. She told me 'He really cares about me. He's such a good guy. I don't know any guys like him.' Girls like us, sometimes we get really convinced by that type of act because we're used to a certain type of jerk, so you meet a guy who's not a drug addict and tucks his shirt in, he seems like a real winner. Now she's off with him. She's at HDT."

"So you're saying he's with Hil and that means trouble."

"I'm saying that if he has anything to do with Hil disappearing, then she is in trouble."

ELEVEN

"Please take that off your Screen," Ronnie said as RIFF23 rolled into the living room playing Groucho glasses.

"I'm undercover," RIFF23 explained.

"Colin's a bad influence on you."

"Unfair, man." Colin lay on the couch wearing one shoe, his shoeless foot propped on the arm of the couch while the other sat flat on the ground.

"You need to go!" Gret said as she entered the room. Her presence reminded Colin of the task at hand. He sat up and started putting on the other shoe.

They were supposed to go to a party and gather information. According to Gret, this Johns guy would probably be there. She was "almost 100% sure."

What with her dramatic opening gesture of showing up at his apartment, in the flesh, unannounced, Ronnie was pretty underwhelmed by Gret's plan, but a plan was a plan and it was better than sitting at home straining his eyes for hours on end by staring at his Screen, hoping to stumble on some sort of clue.

VS parties were hard to get into and packed with beautiful and powerful people. Since Ronnie, Colin, and RIFF23 could be described as neither beautiful nor powerful, Gret was tasked with creating reasonable excuses for them to gain access. She decided the only convincing reason for them to attend the party would be if they were serving food.

"I feel like I'm in *Mission Impossible*," Colin said, carefully adjusting his bowtie.

"Which one?" Ronnie asked.

"17 of course. This is basically exactly what they do to hunt down the hacking conglomerate."

"Remember in 23 when the hacking conglomerate are the good guys?"

"It all goes in cycles, man. Hackers are evil again. I'm sure the next one will have at least one hacker who gets righteously offed."

"God, how have you watched 23-something versions of the same movie?" Gret interrupted.

Colin and Ronnie looked at each other and rolled their eyes.

"No one watches all of the movies," Ronnie explained. "Everyone knows to only watch 1, 4, 14, 17, and 23."

"Well, someone had to watch all of them or who else would be telling you which ones you should watch?" she asked.

They didn't have an answer.

#

They took Ronnie's CAR to a gated neighborhood. RIFF23 fed their credentials to the Robots are Guarding (RAG) model before they were allowed access. As they wound their way down pristine streets, past monstrous houses, Ronnie had the greedy, hopeful feeling he always got when faced with exorbitant wealth–an almost overwhelming need for money. In these situations his mind would run through a list of his talents and assets, desperately seeking some sort of combination that would line up like three cherries, making him rich with ease. Hard work was never part of these mental equations, while a henceforth unknown and childless billionaire relative often appeared.

The party was at the home of Field, the newest VP at the company. Field was obsessed with the television show *Buffy the Vampire Slayer*, and his home décor and lifestyle demonstrated his fandom. His yard was an exact replica of the Sunnydale graveyard. The inside of his house was more generically vampire-related, with lots of red velvet. Instead of the typical expensive, carefully cultivated art collection, the walls in Field's a house were covered with oil paintings of various characters. A particularly large one of Sarah Michelle Gellar greeted visitors in the foyer. Ronnie, Colin, and RIFF23 shouldn't have seen this painting at all, but unacquainted with the ways of the rich, they walked casually into the main entrance before a RAS model quickly directed them to the servants' entrance.

In the kitchen, they were thrown in with the nameless ranks of tuxedoed waiters. Colin was in charge of circulating roasted garlic, Ronnie red wine, and RIFF23 was told to scan the room for nonverbal cues suggesting hunger or a need for attention.

Appetizers were served in a room made to look like a crypt, with stone floors and walls, no windows, and several miniature coffins for seats. The idea of sitting on coffins, no matter how miniature, did not seem to appeal to the party guests, who stood in little clumps, whispering as though they feared waking the dead.

Ronnie walked around distributing the wine in what he assumed was a waiterly fashion. He found it easy to adopt the necessary sycophantic attitude for the job, since he was truly impressed by all the beautiful, rich people shivering in the cold crypt, and was sure they were better than him in every way. Colin was more convincing as a waiter with his stonery, slovenly looks, but less convincing as a servant since he talked in a distracted, aloof tone to the party attendees, often walked right by people as they reached for one of his appetizers, and frequently went into darkened corners to eat a few himself.

RIFF23 stood at attention in the center of the room and summoned waiters through earpieces whenever an individual looked hungry or needy. The uncomfortable nature of the room made it difficult for him to read body language since everyone was looking around impatiently and frowning.

Gret arrived fifteen minutes into the appetizers. She briefly made eye contact with Ronnie before looking around the room, nodding and smiling at people she knew. A few guests came up for hugs and kisses. Ronnie noticed Colin staring in her direction, pieces of garlic starting to slide off of his loosely held platter, until he walked over and snapped in his face.

"Please get it together," Ronnie hissed, then handed Gret a drink per the instructions buzzing in his ear from RIFF23: "The lovely lady in black appears parched."

Dinner was announced. The party moved to the dining room. Ronnie was in the middle of pouring sparkling water for a VS executive's wife when the double doors to the dining room burst open and he saw a face that made his stomach turn.

The man grinned broadly, opened his arms toward everyone in the room, and said, "Sorry I'm late, guys. I had some crimes to commit." There was a large amount of laughter before Field said: "Thanks for gracing us with your presence, Johns."

Johns sat. Ronnie stood clenching the water pitcher to his chest. "Pour him a drink!" RIFF23 hissed through his earpiece.

He walked over slowly and poured the water into Johns' glass. Johns was talking to the woman beside him, but turned just as Ronnie finished. "Thank you, my man," he said in the jovial way rich people use to show they are down to Earth. He grinned, then something in his face shifted. He stared at Ronnie for a moment, raising an eyebrow, before his attention was called away by the young woman next to him.

Did Johns recognize Ronnie? It never occurred to him as a risk, which he now realized was stupid. If Hil was with HDT and met Johns, if he was a remotely nosy person, if she told or was coerced into telling anything about her personal life, then Johns could have looked Ronnie up. Could have seen one of the thousands of pictures of Ronnie's big dumb face that were publicly viewable. He could even be friends with Hil. She could have shared everything with him during a late night stake out. Maybe she told him about their recent arguments. Maybe he comforted her, told her Ronnie sounded like a jerk.

The longer she was gone, the more the strokes of Ronnie's concern were broad and abstract. The disappearance of Hil was a problem to be solved, a puzzle. There were stories he told himself, pieces he tried to fit together, but Hil was lost in these. He failed to consider her daily life, her existence, the idea that she still walked around, talked to people, laughed, cried, and sweat.

He pushed away the thought of her voice going into this stranger's ears, of her smiling and breathing and biting her fingernails in his presence. Then another thought came to him. Maybe there was nothing more to her note than what it said: "Don't try to find me." Maybe she was happy. Maybe she was where she wanted to be. Maybe the whole thing was her way of getting away from Ronnie for good: disappearing, knowing he would fail to find her, banking on his incompetence.

He left the dining room abruptly, setting his tray down next to Johns' place. Colin followed him into the kitchen.

"What are you doing, man?" he asked as their boss came up, yelling, asking what in the hell, exactly, was going on.

"This job isn't for me," Ronnie said. He walked out of the servants' entrance.

"He left his... um... I'll be right back," Colin said and ran out after him. He caught up to Ronnie as he was getting into the CAR.

"Dude. What the hell?" was all he could muster.

"I think Johns recognized me," Ronnie said.

"Fuck."

Ronnie nodded. "Plus... I don't know. I don't know about this plan."

"We don't have much else besides this plan."

"I mean all of it. The whole thing. Trying to find Hil."

"That's cold, bro."

"Is it? Maybe she's where she wants to be."

"You remember her place? Remember how they destroyed her RIFF and all of that? That's not something that happens to someone who is going some place by choice."

Ronnie shrugged. "Maybe she faked it."

"She faked it? She tore up her own house." Colin paused for a second, narrowed his eyes at Ronnie. "Why?"

"To get away from me."

Colin whistled. "Look. I don't want to mess this plan up, so I'm going back inside, but you stay out here and think about what you're saying."

He lay down in the back seat of the CAR, took off his tuxedo jacket, made it into a pillow, and squeezed his eyes shut. All he could think of was Hil, in the woods, starting a revolution, forgetting about him. The note was nothing more than a pity farewell. She had thrown him a bone, basically, something to let him down easy, so he wouldn't blame himself during the lonely nights he faced while she made a new life. She hated him now. He could feel it. She wasn't coming back.

"She isn't coming back," he said to the silent CAR.

"Back up?" the CAR responded.

"Cancel," Ronnie said, sniffling. He pushed hard into his eyes with the palms of his hands, took deep breaths, shook his head, said, "Stop, stop, stop."

"We are stopped," the CAR responded.

"Shut up!" Ronnie yelled.

"OK," the CAR said. The welcoming, happy face on the dash turned to a frown.

Ronnie didn't apologize. He wanted the CAR to be miserable like him.

He tried to focus on the things Colin had said. Why would Hil destroy her own things? Why would she fake being kidnapped? Surely breaking up with Ronnie would be easier than joining a terrorist organization. And what about her parents? They hadn't heard from her either. No matter how she felt about him, Hil loved her parents and wouldn't want to cause them pain. Then again, maybe the Mills were in on it. They seemed to be holding up pretty well for parents with a disappeared daughter.

He fell asleep. He dreamed he was in a small, dark, near-empty room. The walls and floor were an almost black wood. He faced a plain, round table, upon which sat a lamp with a red shade. The lamp cast a red glow over the room. Above the lamp hung a painting. Ronnie knew the painting was called *Hilary Francesca*.

Ronnie never knew what to make of it. Hil mentioned it casually on their second date. He assumed she wanted him to go home and look it up. He did.

In the center of the painting stood a small girl with black hair. Dense woods surrounded her. Sunlight trickled down in front of the girl, but the woods crowded in behind her, so that the further back the painting went, the blacker it got. The girl faced the front, her arms limp at her sides, her face was not set, but seemed in transition, it was as if she saw someone approaching who she almost recognized but could not be sure. She wore a tan cape and black boots. Her fingernails were cherry red and her black hair was cut in a blunt bob that ended at her shoulders, long straight bangs curving into her large, brown eyes.

In his dream, Ronnie approached the painting with his hand extended. He reached out to feel the texture of the leaves. Just before his fingers touched the canvas, he felt a tap on his shoulder. He jumped and spun around. Hil was standing behind him, but it wasn't Hil. Well, it was. The body behind him belonged to the other Hil, Hil from The Believers, Hil 2, but the way she held herself, the look in her eyes, and, when she began to speak, her voice, belonged to Hil 1, his Hil.

"Be careful," the Hils said.

"Of what?" Ronnie asked.

The Hils shook their head, and reached out a hand to stroke Ronnie's face.

"Ronnie," the Hils said.

"Ronnie," a different voice said, more urgently.

Ronnie woke up to see Gret banging on the CAR window, Colin and RIFF23 standing behind her.

"Ronnie! Let us in!" she yelled.

He sat up, shook his head quickly, and said, "Unlock."

The three tumbled into the CAR.

"Go, please," RIFF23 said, and they rolled out into the night, down the winding driveway.

#

"I think Johns knows," Gret said quietly.

The CAR curved down the neighborhood's streets, intermittently dappled with streetlight, uniform houses passing the windows like the world's most boring flipbook.

"Knows what?" Ronnie asked.

"Knows... I don't know... knows we were up to something... or at least me. But I think he figured out. I think he knew already something about all of us. All four of us."

"It was stupid of us to think he wouldn't know me," Ronnie said.

"Yeah," they all answered.

"So, what happened?"

#

After dinner, Field invited the party to take a walk in the cemetery. Gret strolled with him, a few steps behind Johns and another VS girl. She heard through the rumor mill that Johns and Field were friends and were lately into what they called "going on adventures," which was just an obnoxious way of saying traveling to poor countries and staying in huts.

"Have you two been on any adventures lately?" she asked.

Field shrugged. Shook his head. He didn't seem to find it odd that she knew about their adventures, seemed to find it right that she be interested. "Not for a while. Johns has been busy with work."

"Since when does Johns work?" she scoffed.

"Oh he got hired on a few months ago."

"Hired on? You mean, with us?"

Field nodded.

"That's kind of weird."

"Is it? Now you see this is the most well known crypt. Spike lived here."

"Uh-huh. So what does he do for VS?"

"He's a consultant."

"What does that mean?"

"He consults."

The woman walking with Johns peeled away to look inside Spike's crypt. Johns slowed down and waited for the pair to catch up.

"Nice to see you, Gret," Johns said. He kissed her cheeks.

"I hear you're a fellow employee now."

His face went blank for a second. He looked at Field, looked back at Gret, smiled, said: "It's weird one of your clients was here tonight."

"Yeah," Gret's voice came out an octave higher than usual. She cleared her throat. "Yeah that was weird."

"Did he try to talk to you?"

She shrugged. "No. Except to ask if I wanted more wine."

"Wow. That's impressive. A recently deauthorized client sees you and acts totally normal."

"That's true. I have so many I sometimes forget, but you're right. He is deauthorized."

"And I could be wrong, but I'm pretty sure his companion was here too."

She rubbed a hand against a headstone, nonchalant. "Can't say I do much interaction with client companions, so I really couldn't tell you. How is it that you know so much about my client?"

"Ex-client."

"Ex-client. Right."

"It's just part of my job."

"Which is what exactly?"

"Seems like nothing but play to me," Field chimed in, seemingly oblivious to the tone of the conversation. "He gets to travel on the company dime. I'm supposedly important around here and all I ever seem to do is sit in my office."

Just then, Colin came by with a tray. "You want a smoothie?" he asked.

"What's in them?" Field asked.

Gret was holding her breath, wondering if Johns knew something about Colin too.

Colin shrugged. "Quinoa or something."

Johns took a smoothie off the tray and threw it against a nearby headstone.

"Alright, man. Just a 'no' would have been fine," Colin said.

Johns hurried off down the trail.

Field, still oblivious, said: "Johns is a picky eater."

Gret looked for Patty. Patty worked in HR and didn't typically associate with the girls, but during one interminable staff training day she and Gret locked eyes just as Field made a ludicrous statement, and shared the all important eye roll. From then on they had the kind of work friendship that is based solely in negativity. They could talk for hours about how stupid the bosses were, how incompetent their coworkers, but the minute they tried to have a normal conversation, things dried up. "So what's new with you?" Gret would ask. "Oh. You know..." Patty would say, "Same old same."

Patty was drunk, sitting on a cement bench, scrolling absently through her Screen.

"This party sucks," Gret said, sitting beside her.

Patty chuckled, pulled her Screen out, leaned her head against Gret's and took ten selfies. "I don't know what *Buffy* is," she said.

"You know who I just saw?" Gret asked. "Johns. What an asshole."

"Gross. I know. But also, not gross, because he is very cute."

Gret shrugged. "If you say so."

They were silent for a few seconds. Patty leaned in for a few more selfies, this time sticking her tongue out.

"He works here now?" Gret half asked, half stated.

"Yeah. I guess he just couldn't get enough."

"Enough what?"

Patty chuckled.

"What does he do?"

"Says he's a consultant. Seems like he mostly just travels around for 'research' and we pay for it."

"Like... where does he go?"

"All kinds of places. Last week he went to some hippie commune."

"What?"

"Yeah some place called... God, it had the dumbest name. Some place for stoners." She rested her head against Gret's shoulder. Gret expected her to lift up her Screen for another series of selfies, but she seemed to fall asleep.

"Patty?"

Patty sat up quickly. Shook her head back and forth. "God I hate this party."

"Where were you saying Johns went?"

"Oh yeah. It was called... Dope something." She twirled a hand in the air by her head, as if the words might be stirred out. "Doper's Memory. That's what it was."

TWELVE

I did not have secrets. Not the kind that float around your aqueous humor and glimmer at the wrong set of words. I did not have restless sleep and hot-breathed confessions. What I had, leaking from my pulmonary valve, pulling back in time, resisting the move through my body and to my brain, were things I did not want to remember, things I preferred not to know.

When I was seven on the playground I was irritated and told Chele she smelled like garbage. I watched her happy face change, her smiling lips close, her sparkling eyes darken, and in that moment I realized I had the power to change a person. I took a tiny piece of what she was away.

I once sat outside a café and watched an old man struggle to carry groceries to his CAR. He was a parenthesis, his face determined but tired. His bag tipped and an orange rolled down the street. He set his bags down and walked after it.

What grabbed at my throat and stirred my brain were the hands of my past. Not just my past particularly, but that inherited past we don't want but can't escape: The Things Our Parents Did.

I thought my parents were perfect. My teachers and classmates always referred to my father in worshipful tones. At social functions, grownups gathered around my parents and laughed dramatically at their stories.

My life was a self-fulfilling prophecy. My parents raised me to believe that they were good people, that they were special and doing something important. Everyone around me seemed to feel the same way. I knew nothing of a different world, did not feel a curiosity or an itch. I drifted along in the Way Things Were, until I took the Do Good Trip to Doper's Memory.

Like most social trends, the Do Good Trip came about as a Band-Aid to heal a perceived sociological bullet hole. As communities grew less religious and more insulated from grueling poverty and hunger, the youth became more self-obsessed and less introspective. My generation was called the All Good generation, because it was impossible to get us collectively riled up or concerned about issues. We were taught that things would work out in the end, and our bubble communities filled with people like us–happy people with shelter and food and nice Screens–proved that we were right. This state of near-comatose satisfaction was ideal for the government and corporations, so my generation was left to worry about where best to find entertainment and how to look good in pictures.

Then things started to go south. We were all absorbed in our own worlds. We had our set social groups and we didn't really care about anything else. For the government, this meant voting numbers were the lowest they'd been in the history of democracy. There were some cities in which no one voted in the presidential election, which only required opening iVote and tapping on the photograph of the favored candidate.

The young workforce wasn't interested in meeting quotas or enthused about company values. The approval of management meant nothing to them. They were so secure and sure of the All Goodness of the world that being fired seemed a minor inconvenience. Consumers could no longer be counted on to buy items for a "cause." No one cared about causes.

So there was some sort of Old People Convention where leaders discussed what was to be done about the selfish, listless All Good generation. Never mind that these very same Old People were the ones who sold us the products and ideas that turned us this way in the first place. There were many silly, ineffective ideas that emerged from the OPC: nationwide push notifications every hour that reminded us to "Take a minute and look around. The world is a beautiful place. The world is your home," monthly Eye Opener sessions for grades K-12 in which schools assembled to watch a one hour video feed of an outside group living their life. Nature School, where children were made to sit outside for half an hour a day without a Screen.

The Do Good Trips were a more successful part of the plan. Each year we were bused to some tent community or quarantine village to do some good. We weren't allowed to have our Screens, so everyone experienced days of unimpeded social interaction. I observed how much more natural my classmates acted when they weren't wondering if someone was taking their picture, how much nicer when they weren't hoping to get quoted for some funny remark. And it was good for us to interact with people who were different from us, to see pain and suffering, and even joy and happiness in what we would consider an unlivable situation. On the ride home we were quiet, remembering what we saw, evaluating how to Be Better, how to Do More and realizing that maybe we should take a minute and look around us. The world was a complicated place. The world was our home.

Doper's Memory was an OTG community, self-sustained by a farm and marijuana business. Due to concurrent years of drought and crop failure, the community was struggling. It took a lot of convincing for them to even allow all these On-TG kids to run amok in their community, but their food supplies were dangerously low and there were many critical repairs that needed to be made to compound buildings.

The night we arrived, a man named Leonard greeted us and helped unload food and supplies. Leonard was in his mid-forties with shoulder-length, black hair, wearing a ripped jean jacket and round glasses. He had bright blue eyes that were partially glazed. He patted us on our backs and said things like "Wow, man, look at all these gridders doing good work and stuff."

DM consisted of around 300 residents, most with two parents, many multi-generational, spread across several acres and living in efficient, tiny, wheeled houses. The community was once much larger, but with crop failures, all but the truest OTGers left. There were several empty houses, some of which were used as lodging for our DGT group.

Leonard walked us to our houses as the sun set. All I could see were grass and trees and dirt kicked up by our feet. We were silent, but it was the silence of listening to bugs buzz, birds chirp, the wind rustle the trees, and Leonard hum, not the silence of eyes on Screens. After we chose our beds, I left the house alone to wander the grounds, happily swinging a lantern. As I walked past The Trading Post, I heard someone coughing, and followed the sound around the back of the building.

In the dirt, leaning against a wall, sat a thin girl with wild black hair that came down her back almost to her hips. She was wearing a flimsy white tank top with cut off shorts and no shoes or bra. She raised a joint to her lips and inhaled, holding the dwindling remains out to me. I shrugged and took it, sitting down beside her and breathing in the familiar warmth. "How's the do goodin'?" she finally asked, exhaling. I savored my breathless state for a moment longer before releasing the smoke and answering, "Just got here, haven't done any good yet."

She nodded. She looked about my age, or looked like what people my age would look like if they spent time outside: freckled nose, chapped lips. Her eyes reminded me of someone.

"Are you related to Leonard?" I asked.

"He's my dad," she said.

"Aww. He's so nice."

She shrugged. "Yeah, he's alright."

"So have you always lived here?"

"Born and raised hippie scum." She took a couple more drags and passed the joint back to me. When we were breathing again, I said, "Man, I'm glad I ran into you." I could feel my face becoming dopey and glazed.

"Don't gridders have weed?"

"Well, you guys must have customers, I suppose. I always just get some from my parents, but they don't want me to be a... doper... so they sort of keep it limited."

"Weird. I thought getting the connect from your parents was a very here thing."

"Well," I said, proudly, "my parents are a little out of the ordinary for grid parents I guess." I looked around a minute, took another drag, passed it back. "They'd probably like living in a place like this, actually."

"So why don't they?"

I smiled. It was amusing how simple it was to her. She'd never known anything else, after all. "Well, it's not so easy to just leave a life, I guess. Plus they like to, they're sort of part of the community and all that."

"Got fancy jobs?"

"Well..." It was weird. I both liked and disliked revealing my parentage. I was proud of them, and I liked seeing the awed faces of others, to see that they too thought much of my parents, but I didn't like the chance that the person might start acting weirdly toward me or might only want to talk about my parents for the rest of the conversation. Plus it was a conversation I'd had with so many people so many times that it was almost boring, like reciting a poem learned through rote memorization.

"Are you going to be mysterious all night?" she asked. The joint was finished. She dropped it and put it out with the heel of her foot.

"Sorry," I started, "My parents are the Mills." I was pleasantly high enough that I just sort of grinned and stared at her for a while before I noticed her big blue eyes blinking at me, waiting. "Oh. Hm," I giggled, "I guess you don't learn about them out here. You really should, though, considering."

"Considering?"

"How supportive they are of your way of life."

"Just not supportive enough to live it."

I laughed. "Well, so, my dad is sort of this famous inventor. He invented the Selfie Mirror."

She looked at me with a confused expression.

"It's what it sounds like."

She spit in the dirt.

"Yeah, I know," I continued. "And that's the thing. He feels the same as you. He was young when he invented it and now he regrets it. So my parents are very anti-Tech. We don't have Screens or bots or anything in our house."

"Yeah, mine either."

"Yeah, well, obviously."

"So you are OTG in a way... no Tech... but, what? You still go to school with these normal, narcissistic Tech users? They're your neighbors and friends?"

"There are ways to be part of normal society without Tech."

"Sure. If you're super rich."

I paused. I felt the confusion of my euphoric high and the sharp pain of her words. I tried to remember if anyone in my life had ever bluntly pointed out that my parents were rich. "I don't think it really matters..." I started.

"Sure it does. My dad was OTG for a while before moving out here. Well, first of all he couldn't truly be OTG because he needed a CAR to get to work, and when he ditched the CAR for Public Transit, he still had to have a Profile to use the train. So he deleted his Profile and ditched his Screen and started walking to work, which took about an hour each way, but his work fired him because he had to have a Profile for performance review and he had to use a Screen to clock in. They refused to offer him any sort of accommodation. He could never find a real job after that. Even the lowest, most under the table jobs were done by bots. Plus, his social life completely disintegrated. No one could really contact him unless they showed up at his door. It was too much effort."

"He didn't get a telephone?"

She rolled her eyes. "Do you have any idea how much vintage Tech costs?"

I didn't say anything.

"So eventually he gave up on the whole deal and moved here. I think... I mean we're happy here as a family, but I can tell by the way he talks sometimes about his old life that he misses it. He liked the city and going to work every day for a nine to five shift. He liked his friends. Not that he doesn't have friends here, it's just that here everything is about your beliefs. Dad didn't want to sit around with people and discuss the evils of Tech. He just made a personal choice to be free of it."

We were silent. I watched a worm inch along in my lantern's glow. The things this girl was saying were making me feel sick. She hadn't actually said anything directly against my parents, but it wasn't difficult to get her meaning.

"What's your name?" I asked, finally.

"Isis."

"Hil."

She pushed herself up and stood above me, arms crossed. "Well, Hil, seeing as how my joint's gone and all, my work here is done. I'm going to bed."

"My parents are good people," I said.

"OK," she said, and started to walk off.

"Wait! I'm serious. My dad is just really smart, and he used that smartness to create things. Later, when he learned more about the world, he regretted those inventions, but it was too late to undo them. All he could do was change the way he lived."

"Right. And he still probably makes a ton of money from those choices he regrets. Money, I'm assuming he doesn't turn away. And he's still fully accepted in society. Why? Because he's rich from something he invented, which most of the people he socializes with probably use. To them he's just some eccentric rich guy. He's a genius really, because he gets to have it both ways. Do you think if your dad hadn't famously invented this piece of Tech, if he was just some average guy on the street who wanted to live a more honest life, everyone would still give a shit? Well, I just told you about my dad, so we know the answer." She stopped talking for a moment, but she looked like she wasn't done. I waited. "It's just sort of bullshit that your dad helped create the world that people like us," she motioned around the compound, "are trying to escape, and he gets to pretend like it's easy as pie to get away from it." She walked off. I didn't try to call her back or follow her.

I ran into Isis again toward the end of our trip. I was in Ms. Ellis's loft, looking for a raccoon. Ms. Ellis couldn't climb the ladder anymore. She claimed she heard rustling at night and was sure it was a vengeful raccoon that she once tried to shoot when it got into her garbage.

Since the loft window was wide open, and its floor covered with random paper and photographs, it seemed likely that many creatures rummaged around up there. I shut the window and started looking through some of the photographs. "I'm the raccoon," a voice said. I looked up to see Isis's head at the top of the ladder. She climbed up, cleared a space among the debris, and sat down. "Ms. Ellis keeps everything," she said.

"What is all this?" I asked.

"It's the unofficial history of Doper's Memory." She grabbed some images of smiling, longhaired people in an empty field. "These are some of the founding dopers."

"And these notes?"

"Just different letters, instructions, recipes. All kinds of things."

"And she just keeps all this stuff thrown up here like this?"

"Well, I was helping her with an organization project, and then she fell and hurt her hip. I would come visit her and then come up here to 'work,' but I never really got anywhere with it. I liked seeing everything spread out here. I like that I can just pick something up at random and it could be a photograph of my parents or it could be a receipt for potatoes. Sometimes at night when I can't sleep I climb in the window and look through everything."

"Raccoon."

"Right."

"Having it all scattered and crumpled like this doesn't stress you out?"

"It's sort of like being in the brain of the commune: up in this loft, ideas and memories and facts spread around you, exciting things and boring things. I think this is exactly how it should be kept."

"And what if someone needs to find something?"

"Then they turn into raccoons too."

"Don't you ever want to take some of this to show? To share? I mean especially the pictures of your parents."

"I know about them. I've seen them hundreds of times. My parents were there when they were taken. Who else needs to know?"

I didn't have an answer. "Whatever, just stop coming here at night and I'll tell her I caught the raccoon."

She laughed. "'Whatever' back at you."

I was done with my duties for the day, so we wandered around the compound as the sun set. "I hope I didn't upset you the other day," she said.

"No you don't."

"I guess you're right. I meant to upset you. But I think I like you, so I hope you being upset doesn't make us not friends."

"It's weird. I like you too."

"What's so weird about that?"

"Well you're kind of a bitch."

"Oh that's just what people say when you have an opinion and you share it."

"Is that what your mother told you the first time someone called you a bitch?"

She just smiled.

We were quiet for a while, itching bug bites and watching commune dwellers sitting on porches and kids kicking up dirt. "I wasn't being completely straight with you before," Isis said.

"What? You aren't a raccoon?"

"No. Before before."

"Oh. You love Selfie Mirrors?"

"I don't like you."

"I have an opinion and I share it."

"When I first met you. I didn't realize it right away, but then I did... I knew who you were. I know who your parents are."

"How?"

"The photographs."

THIRTEEN

The gang decided to get appropriately high on the ride up to Doper's Memory. RIFF23 asked Ronnie to reprogram his logic and time sensors so he could be included. It was fun for the humans, but not RIFF23, who kept saying "We should be there by now" and "Where are we going again?" The only emoji he would play was a pot leaf, and whenever he remembered that was what he was doing, he would say "Hey! Guys! Look!" and let out his weird, robot laugh.

Doper's Memory did not match the photographs online: happy, bright little houses, dirt roads, quaint stores. The gate through which they entered had a rusted arch with the compound's name outlined in iron, a sad welcome. The paint on the houses was peeling, the streets abandoned, the Trading Post—from which Gret had hoped to buy a souvenir t-shirt— boarded up. Their highs turned against them.

"What is going on here, man?" Colin asked, darting his eyes back and forth. "I'm freaking out!" RIFF23 said. Ronnie quickly adjusted his settings back to normal. "Calm down," Gret said. "That woman we talked to told us it was going to be like this. Sort of. Well, she said it's not like how it used to be. I wasn't exactly sure what that meant, but she said it in sort of a foreboding tone."

"Like a spooky witch?" Colin shouted.

After following a few of the branching, dusty roads, they stopped, per instructions, at a bright blue house. It offered a stark contrast to the neighboring houses, which were caving in and dingy. A woman with long, black hair, dressed in cut offs and a Rolling Stones t-shirt, answered the door.

"Yeah?" she said.

"Are you Isis?" Gret asked.

"Yeah. Gret?"

"Yep!"

Without saying anything else, she turned and walked into the house, leaving the door open behind her. The four looked at each other and shrugged, except RIFF23, who played a bouncing question mark emoji. They walked in behind her. "I like your shirt!" Ronnie called toward her back. Gret rolled her eyes.

"I don't want to go in there, man," Colin whispered loudly to Gret. She shoved him through the door.

Isis sat at her kitchen table and motioned lazily for them to join her. The table, a padded bench, and an L-shaped counter with a tiny stove and refrigerator were all that fit in the downstairs of the house. There was a ladder leading up to a loft where, Ronnie assumed, she slept. It was a clean, cheerful room with bright, yellow walls, but very impersonal, not a knick-knack or framed photo in sight.

"Do you have a Screen?" Ronnie asked, looking around.

Colin giggled uncontrollably. Gret hit his arm.

"It's a reasonable question. I mean, Hil had one after all," Ronnie stopped, looking at Isis. "Oh, Hil was my..."

"I know who Hil is," she said, "and of course she has a Screen. Figures. She never really was one of us."

"How do you know Hil?" Ronnie asked.

"Weird question. I thought you were here about Hil. When Gret called she said something about her boyfriend, but same difference."

"I hate when people say 'same difference,'" RIFF23 said.

"Not important!" Ronnie said.

"Do you have a Screen?" RIFF23 asked in his Ronnie voice, which was exaggeratedly slowed down and low and sort of sounded like those things serial killers use to disguise their voices when making threatening phone calls.

"This little guy's a trip!" Isis said.

"I guess you don't see a lot of robots," Gret said.

"Definitely not. It's actually a charter rule to immediately dismantle any robot that crosses onto the commune."

Everyone was silent. Colin's eyes were wide and unblinking. RIFF23 played no emoji.

"Just kidding! Well... not really, but I'm the only one here now and I don't feel like following the charter. Too much work."

"Yeah, so, anyway," Ronnie started. "Like you were saying, I'm Hil's boyfriend, and we..."

"You?" Isis asked.

"Yeah. Me. I guess Gret explained when she contacted..."

"I didn't mention you or Hil," Gret interrupted, looking puzzled.

"No. Yeah. You talked about Johns. Hil's boyfriend."

Ronnie got up and left the house. The sun was at its daily peak, and he broke out into a sweat as he ambled down Isis's street. He'd been right all along. Everyone said he was paranoid, and he was paranoid, but he had this annoying friend in high school who liked to say "Just because you're paranoid doesn't mean they're not out to get you," and as much as he hated it when his friend said that, as much as he really hated it when his friend wore a shirt that said that, it was a tenet, he was learning, that held true.

Sure, it was paranoid to think that a terrorist group abducted your girlfriend, but, turns out, true. It was paranoid to think that the government and corporations were spying on you, but again, very true. It was especially paranoid to think that said girlfriend would become a willing member of said terrorist group along with the son of the director of the NSA of said government and employee of one of said corporations, and that this girlfriend and this son would end up falling in love as they blew stuff up together, but there he sat in Isis's tiny house learning another paranoid truth.

It was strange how Hil's person could change, the version he kept with him. Now she was a blank face, a stranger. He wanted to go back in time, to record everything they ever said to each other, to find her now, to sit her down and make her listen, to say to her "You and me, remember? You love me, don't you recall? You said so that time I told you the story of how I broke my leg in second grade when my brother threw a stick through the spokes of my bike." He heard someone calling his name, and turned to see Gret, running up behind him.

"Ronnie, I know you're upset, but..."

"No. I'm fine," he cut her off.

"No you're not."

He shrugged.

"Either way, we don't really know this Isis person, and I don't want to take up a ton of her time, so let's go find out what she has to say so we can leave."

"I'm sure she's really busy out here," he said.

Isis was pouring tea for Colin. "She's making me trippy tea!" he said, excitedly.

"I guess she's not a witch anymore," Ronnie said.

Colin shrugged.

"How long does it take to work?" Ronnie asked.

"About half an hour," Isis said.

"Well, then, pour us all some and talk fast."

Isis, born and raised in Doper's Memory, did not talk fast. She talked slowly and often went down several unrelated conversational paths before returning to her subject, but she did her best. When she first met Hil, Hil was 17 and she was 16. Hil was at DM for some dopey straight world thing where they helped sad, poor people, and felt better about themselves.

"Damn. They got to do their DGT here?" Colin interrupted. "We always had to go to an old folk's home and clean the toilet."

So, she and Hil got close on this trip and Hil told her about her boyfriend, Johns, who was some senator's son or something and sounded like sort of a jerk to Isis, not that anyone asked her opinion, but sometimes Hil would ask and she'd say "He's a jerk!" and they'd both move on.

"Wait," Ronnie said, standing up and sloshing tea on his shirt. "She knew Johns already?"

RIFF23 starting spinning around the room, playing an emoji of a wide-eyed face biting its fingernails. "What is going on?" His speakers chirped with his high pitch.

"Did someone adjust him again?" Ronnie asked.

"He asked me to," Isis said. "Now let me finish."

So after that summer Isis and Hil started writing each other letters, and Hil would come visit every summer and stay for a few weeks. Isis even ventured into the straight world and stayed with the Mills a few times, which was not that bad. She only met Johns once. Hil brought him to stay with her at DM one summer, but he was only there for a few hours before they had a huge fight and he left. "Hil told me they broke up a few years ago," Isis said. "She was dating some nice-sounding dork... I guess that would be you."

Ronnie only sipped on his tea in response.

"Anyway, I haven't heard from her in a while... a couple of months... happens sometimes. People get busy. Then when Johns showed up here, told me they were back together, said she sent him to destroy the chip... Normally I'd be skeptical, but he knew way too much about the chip to have heard about it from anyone other than Hil."

"What chip?" Ronnie asked. "I'm so confused."

"I know you are," Isis said, patting his hand. "Drink your tea."

He gulped down the rest. She followed suit. Gret and Colin, based on their wide eyes and stupid grins, had finished theirs a while ago.

"Are you going to tell me or what?" Ronnie asked.

"Tell you what?"

"You know!"

"The thing is, Hil made you sound really nice. I hated Johns, but no one else seemed to see what I saw."

"I know, right?" Gret said. She had her head on Colin's shoulder.

"It all started when I was 16. Hil was 17, and she was visiting on some sort of straight world trip where..."

Colin had a hysterical outburst, before finally gathering himself and saying "Yeah. You told us that part."

"Oh. What part did I not tell you?"

"The part about the chip!" Ronnie yelled.

"If you're going to be unchill, then I can't tell you anything," she said, crossing her arms.

"Sorry. I'm not unchill. I'm chill! I promise."

"So how does the part about the chip go?" Isis sipped her tea, thoughtfully, for a few seconds, and stared out a window behind Ronnie's head. "I knew who she was, of course."

"You know about people like the Mills here?" Gret asked.

"Gret. Please don't encourage her," Ronnie interrupted. "Isis. The chip..."

"This is about the chip, man," Isis said.

"Yeah, man," Colin said.

"Fine, man," Ronnie said.

"So, no, Gret, we don't normally know about people like the Mills, but I knew her. I looked at her picture every day."

"A picture of Hil?" Ronnie asked. "What are you *talking* about?"

"Hold on!" Isis said. She stood up quickly, took a second to steady herself, then raced up the ladder to her loft. The four visitors were silent downstairs, listening to her heavy footsteps and the sound of items being thrown around, some landing with a soft pat, others with loud thumps. "Found it!" she yelled, descending the ladder with something tucked under her arm. When she got to the bottom, she held it out in front of her, as far away from her body as possible, as though the object held something that would infect her if it touched her chest. It was a small, dusty picture frame. Inside was a photograph of Hil.

#

A few times, at the Mills' house, Laura pulled out a big book of photographs and showed them to Ronnie while Hil complained.

The one Isis held in front of her, striped by the setting sun filtering in through the windows, was one of his favorites. It featured Hil at the height of awkward teen girldom. Her hair looked slightly greasy–parted down the center and cut bluntly below her chin. The radiating hairs of each eyebrow reached for each other over her tiny nose. She smiled a large, joyful grin, displaying yellowing, clear braces. The first time he saw the photograph, it stirred up something new in him; poked at a soft part he didn't know was there. He already loved Hil, and felt tenderness for her, but this was something new–a short glimpse at who she used to be, a sudden understanding of a part of her that was flawed and naïve.

#

"How did you get that?" Ronnie asked. He was standing in front of Isis's outreached arms, tracing a line in the dust on the frame, straight down the center of Hil's face.

"I'll get there," Isis said. Her voice was no longer abstract and flaky-sounding. She was serious. She looked at him sadly and handed him the frame. Ronnie sat down with it hugged to his chest.

"When Hil came here, that picture had been sitting on the counter over there," she motioned to the corner of bare countertop beside the stove, "for a couple of years.

"Before that there was one from when she was maybe six or seven. Before that, I was too young to remember, but I'm guessing there was some sort of naked baby picture or something. Same deal with her parents. There'd be a picture of them, always left up for five to ten years, then changed out as they aged a little."

"How'd you get them?" Ronnie asked again.

"How'd she get them?" Gret interjected, bewildered. "Ronnie, aren't you curious why they had them in the first place?"

"Yeah. That too," Ronnie said. There were too many questions for him to figure out how they ranked in importance.

"We're really not so different from the clichés here, you know," Isis said.

"Here we go," Ronnie sighed, sipping his tea.

"Just let her be," Colin said. He smiled dopily, eyes wide.

"What I mean is like, here on the compound, we have—well we had at least—an oral history tradition. And written too. Well, we tried to do written, but whoever was in charge of it would always forget to keep writing, so if you read our compound history, it's in fits and starts, a few years missing here, a decade there. But for people who forget a lot, who forget to do things, that is, we don't *forget* forget. We remember our stories. Sort of. We remember the general idea of our stories."

"Promising," Ronnie said.

"The things I tell you will be true in the ways that are important," Isis said, looking at him steadily.

"Just not true in ways that are true?" he asked.

"Emotionally, it will all be true. Some of the details might be mixed up."

Ronnie said nothing. He returned her look. He tried to convince himself that he saw wisdom, that she knew something vital that would save Hil. She hiccupped.

"Hil was basically famous when she came here. Well, that version of Hil, at least." She motioned toward the picture frame, laying face up in Ronnie's lap. "When I met her, I kept thinking I knew her, but it took a few days to figure it out. She was through puberty. She was very beautiful. She only looked like the girl in the picture when she was really happy, and did that exact same dorky grin, minus the braces.

"So once, like, I guess thirty or so years ago, this couple moved here. No one knew much about them, where they came from, what they did, and here it's not like anyone's going to look it up or anything. So they came and they fit in right away, and became very popular, sort of leaders of the pack. They were mechanically minded and helped fix things, built little machines that made things easier. They were funny and attractive and entertaining. They quickly became the center of commune social life.

"Then one day, someone caught the man taking their picture. This was disturbing on many levels to the populace of Doper's Memory. First of all, surreptitious picture-taking was generally frowned upon. Second of all, the person whose photograph was taken claimed that she saw him taking it with a Screen."

Colin, lying on the floor, staring at the ceiling, gasped. Ronnie giggled. Gret kicked each of them. RIFF23 said, "Could someone adjust me back? I'm starting to think Isis is a witch."

Ronnie obliged.

"Screens here are a big no no of course. The man denied it up and down. Said this woman was crazy. Didn't just say that he didn't take her picture with a Screen, said he didn't take her picture at all, that she must have been hallucinating or something. Most people wanted to believe him, and it seems like his accuser wasn't too popular, so for a while the matter was dropped. Then a second accusation came in. This person claimed that they caught the woman listening under their window to a private conversation: crouched down on the ground like a spy. They said she had something in her hand, which she hid very quickly, but they were pretty sure it was a Screen. From there, the whole situation got Salem Witched. Everyone had seen them in the wrong place doing the wrong thing.

"Eventually there was a hearing. Now everything here is not really in line with the law. We try to maintain order and all that, be good people, but there aren't subpoenas or search warrants or whatever. There's no fair trial by a jury of your peers. At the hearing, all 300-something residents of Doper's Memory got to vote on what they wanted to do, and they voted unanimously (minus the family in question, of course) to search and seize their property. Lest they be able to clean anything out, they were held in protective custody in the Trading Post while this went on. What they found was not good. Their house had a false wall in the back closet that went into a small, extra room. In this room was a Screen on which they found file after disturbing file. There were secret photographs of every single member of the commune, even photographs of ultrasounds for the unborn members. There were recordings of private conversations. There were hours of video footage of day-to-day life.

"When asked why they'd done it, the couple shrugged and smiled. They refused to answer. They said they would leave peacefully and never come back. Most other places probably wouldn't have let them leave just like that, but this isn't like most other places. So the people sighed and said 'OK,' and let them leave.

"So those people were the Mills. The incident really hit DM hard. We were such a tight-knit community, and a sense of trust is the foundation of this sort of place. So the story of the Mills became one of our town tales. It was a reminder that people lie, that we trick each other, that we can't be too trusting, but also that we love one another. That we forgive. The Mills sent my dad pictures every few years. He wanted to remember them, to see them as they aged and changed, and when they had Hil, he asked for pictures of her too."

"And you never found out what they were up to?" Ronnie asked. He was now lying on Isis's bench, with one foot on the floor to try to prevent the room from spinning.

"The compound never found out, but I pieced it together from what Bill told my dad, and what Hil found out.

"They were working on a project for the government. Some sort of Artificial Intelligence that could instantly gather all data about a person for one complete profile–all their likes and dislikes, shopping habits, relationships, crimes, presence in crime-related areas, flagged conversations, that sort of stuff.

"I guess they weren't satisfied with the fact that this software would work on the general population who automatically opted-in for having their personal information mined and used against them. They wanted people like us, who made an effort to not share ourselves with the whole world, to be part of this project too. So they chose DM as an experimental site to set up a model for other developers who could travel around the world to all OTG compounds and record our conversations, take our photographs, take detailed notes about our personalities and lives, to be entered into this endless government and corporate data banks."

"So," Ronnie started, his eyes closed, "when Hil came here, her parents didn't warn her or anything that everyone would know who she was?"

"No. She didn't know anything about it. She didn't know they had been here, she didn't know about the project."

"Isn't it sort of a crazy coincidence that this is the place she ended up coming for her DGT?" Gret asked.

"It would seem so, but Hil figured out later, when she talked to her parents, that they set the whole thing up. Basically, it was eating them up to keep this secret from her, but they were too scared to tell her, so they convinced the school to do the DGT here."

"So what about Johns?" Ronnie asked.

"Johns?"

"Why did he come here?"

"Oh! To get the chip!"

"Back to the damn chip."

"Yeah. He told me Hil wanted to destroy the chip."

"Isis. Please. What is the chip?"

"I could go for some chips," Colin said.

"My dad loved Bill. The whole thing was really hard for him. Bill was his best friend, pretty much, and it was mostly his idea–the whole sending pictures thing. Dad was Bill's right-hand man. They did a lot of projects together. They smoked a lot of weed together. They would sit out front of the Trading Post at night and other communers would come by and everyone would chat and laugh. One of the best and worst things about my dad is his honesty. The man couldn't tell a lie, unless he couldn't remember the truth. He was good for Bill. Bill tends to inspire this sort of worshipful attitude in people–even egalitarian potheads. So it was good for him to have someone who didn't laugh when he told a dumb joke and challenged him on his opinions.

"A couple of years after the Mills left for good, Bill wrote my dad a letter and they met up on some dirt road outside the compound. Bill said he'd decided to give it all up. He was quitting the project for the government. He had this chip. It had all his work on it from the past, I don't know, ten years or whatever. He asked my dad to hide it from him. He said he knew he should destroy it, but he couldn't bring himself to do it.

"He just needed to trust that my dad had it and would keep it safe and hidden, and never tell anyone about it. Then whenever they both died, no one would ever know where it was and it would be gone for good. It was an OK plan. I mean it was a stupid plan, but it seemed like it could work. Except my dad wasn't the world's best secret keeper. I guess that's obvious, since I'm telling you this story and it was supposed to be a secret. One summer when Hil was visiting, we all shared a pot of this very same tea, and he accidentally told us everything. He had buried the chip in a box behind our house, under a blueberry bush.

"The next day when he realized what he'd done, he was very upset. He didn't like breaking promises. He cried and said he would never drink tea again and he made us both promise to keep the secret." Isis began to cry. The four of them sat in silence, unsure how to comfort a stranger. RIFF23 played a frowning emoji.

"Sorry," she said finally, blowing her nose loudly, "I just miss him. It's hardest when I think about him at a time like that, when he was sad. He was a really kind person."

Ronnie felt too awkward to ask what happened to her dad. He opted for making a commiserative noise. They were quiet for a while. Gret and Colin were lying on the floor, side by side, holding hands, staring at the ceiling. Ronnie sat on Isis's bench, knees pulled under his chin, rocking back and forth.

#

That night, Ronnie had a vision. It happened sometime after Colin starting telling them that everything around him was made of triangles–that even they were triangles, but he was a circle, and the degree to which this was causing him to freak out, when Gret interrupted, calmly, and said that no, she was a circle too.

Hil came to him. He was lying uncomfortably on Isis's bench. She stood over him, dressed in her sunflowers, hair the wild way it was when she got out of the shower and went on with her day. Her face was different. She looked tired, sadder

141

than he remembered, things she didn't want to know, or didn't want to remember, hidden somewhere behind her steady gaze. He reached out to touch the bags under her eyes, but she took his hand in hers before he reached them, kissed his knuckles, and said, "Follow me." He sat up and noticed that she wasn't wearing any shoes. Her toenails were a chipped pink, the bottoms of her feet, he noticed as she walked toward the door, dirty. "Am I tripping?" he asked. She shrugged and pushed her way outside.

He scrambled up and ran after her. He couldn't see her anywhere. At first he panicked, then noticed her footprints on the dirt road. He thought she'd only had a few seconds' head start, but he walked and walked and still did not find her. Eventually, he reached the sad, iron gate that marked DM's entrance, and walked out of the compound. Hil's feet led him to a field of dead, brown grass. Her tracks ended, but he hoped if he kept walking straight he would find her. He was right.

She sat at the edge of the field, just before it broke into underbrush leading to a dense wood. The sun was almost through setting, the trees stark black against the maroon sky. Ronnie sat next to her. She didn't turn or react to his presence. He craned his neck to look at her face. She was crying, silently. He watched tears move slowly down her cheeks and drip from her chin. She reached out for his hand and squeezed.

Ronnie became aware of a terrible sound. It came from nowhere. It was all around them. It was the sound of the world, which was no sound at all. Hil looked at him. She said nothing. Again, he wanted to reach out, press his fingers into the bags under her eyes, smooth the tears making bumpy paths down her face, but he hesitated. The sound was unbearable. It filled him with dread.

When he looked into Hil's eyes, he was a different Ronnie. Years had passed without her. He knew what it was like to have lived without her. She was different and he was different. They had changed, apart, in ways that made them strange to each other. Then time rewound and they were back to Hil and Ronnie in the present. "Did you see it?" Hil asked. She let go of his hand. Ronnie nodded. The redness was almost gone from the sky. All that remained was a small line of bleak light at the bottom of the trees. "Don't let it happen," she said.

Ronnie woke up with dead grass pricking his face. He walked back into the compound, taking wrong turns, circling around, until he found his way back to Isis's house. Gret was sitting on the front step, hair tousled, eye makeup smudged, sipping tea. "More tea?" Ronnie asked.

"This is normal tea," she replied, her voice in that husky stage of first waking.

"Where's everyone else?"

She shrugged. "Inside I guess. I just had to get out of there you know? The whole tiny house thing was just too... tiny."

"Yeah. Me too."

"You have a nice walk?"

"Yeah. I guess."

Inside, Colin was passed out on the floor, and RIFF23 rolled around tidying up. Isis stood over the stove, stirring a big pot. "Oatmeal!" she said, cheerfully. "Did you have a special experience last night?"

"Nah," he said. She walked over to him, held him by the shoulders, and stared into his eyes.

"Hm," she said, suspiciously. "That's strange. My trippy tea is pretty much 100% on the hallucinatory experiences."

"Well, I hate to be the one to stand in the way of statistics, but I just had a nice rest. The colors in my dream might have been a little psychedelic, but that's about it."

"I doubt you had a good night sleep since RIFF23 says you've been gone for hours."

"Gotta love my little spy."

"Spies!" Colin shouted, jumping up and hitting his head on the table. "Where's Gret?"

"And what about you, Colin?" Isis asked. "Any experiences last night?"

"What do you mean?" he asked in a cautious tone.

"Did you trip out, man?" RIFF23 asked, playing a peace sign.

"Well, we know about the triangles already," Isis said. "Anything else happen to expand your consciousness?"

"Oh. Yeah. Yeah. Definitely."

"Well..." she said.

"Oh. Well, I'd rather keep it between myself and my expanded consciousness, if you don't mind. Still working it all out."

"Yeah. Of course. I feel you."

"So, Isis," Ronnie said. "When Johns came here... you said he wanted to destroy the chip. That Hil wanted him to. Did he?"

She looked up from the pot. She shook her head slowly, her eyes widening. "No, Ronnie," she said. She said it like it was the most obvious thing in the world. "No, that's not what happened at all."

He sighed. Shrugged. "Well?"

She threw her hands up. "Stir this, please." She went and sat on the bench.

"He told me... What did he say? My memory's not so good. He said Hil decided to end it, the stuff with her parents, once and for all. She wanted the chip destroyed. I asked him why she sent him instead of coming herself. He and I barely knew each other. 'She's busy,' he said. 'Doing what?' I asked. He said she wrote me a note."

She pulled an envelope out of her back pocket. Ronnie recognized the green lily pad. He grabbed it from her, pulled out the note. Isis returned to stirring the pot.

"*Isis*," he read. "*Sorry I can't be there with you, but things have come up. I'm worried about my parents. I think they might change their minds about the chip. I can't explain why, exactly, just something in their attitudes lately. Dad told me he misses his work. I've never heard him say anything like that. I know you don't really know Johns that well, and I know this is weird, but I need the chip destroyed. The sooner it's done, the sooner I'll have peace of mind. Thank you for understanding. XOXO Hil.*"

"That's not her hand writing," he said.

Isis shook her head. "I guess it isn't. It looked like it to me. I thought it was strange, the note, him being here, but I didn't know what to do, I was alone and he was here, in my house, grinning at me in that weird way he has. So I took him out to the blueberry bush and I dug it up. It was in a little black velvet jewelry box. When I opened it up, I saw the chip, a tiny shiny star, and that was it. I woke up hours later in the dirt. The sun was setting. Johns was gone. The note from Hil was thrown in the hole I dug.

"The thing is I'm glad you said that, that it wasn't her hand writing, because that's what I wanted to believe, but part of me was afraid."

"Of what?"

"Of her. Of her changing. That she wrote that letter and sent him here. Told him to hit me over the head."

"Hil wouldn't..." Ronnie started.

"You don't know," she said. "You can never be sure."

FOURTEEN

The road that ran alongside Doper's Memory was dusty and rutted. An orange haze surrounded the CAR as it slid along, jolting the passengers every few feet. Ronnie looked out at the bristly, dust-tinted trees.

"Pull over," he said.

The CAR obeyed, its low humming dissolving into silence. The dust settled. They sat on a patch of dead grass overlooking a dry ditch, the movements of old rains etched in the dirt as divots and pattern-less lines. Beyond the ditch lay an ugly field of dirt. Some small, brown-furred creature moved out there, steadily, happily, as if it did not know it was being watched or that it walked in a desolate place.

No one spoke. Gret and Ronnie stared out at the field, Colin slept, his head against the window and his mouth open. RIFF23 wore a blank Screen, seated between Gret and Colin in the back seat.

Gret reached up from the backseat and placed a hand on Ronnie's shoulder. "What should we do now?" she asked, her voice starting in a whisper, cracking into normality halfway through.

He shrugged, tapped at the window, asked: "What is that thing?"

No one answered.

"RIFF23?"

"Sorry. I'm still offline. Let me..." his Screen showed a loading bar for a few seconds. "That would be a prairie dog."

"Is it a dog?"

"No it's a rodent... ummm... Hey Ronnie, the timing might be bad but your Entertainment Package just arrived. Do you want to watch it?"

Ronnie nodded. "Drive," he said. The CAR rolled back onto the road. He and Gret leaned in close and experienced the changing sounds and colors coming from the bot. It was the usual stuff. A cat jumped as if pulled by a string at the sight of a cucumber, the week would see a high of 80 degrees and a low of 75, 0% chance of precipitation. The RIFF upgrade patch would be ready to download tomorrow at noon. A person hiding in a box played a series of pranks on b-level celebrities by popping out suddenly.

Then there was this.

"We received word that the headquarters of Internet Movies were bombed at 4:00 a.m. this morning. A bomb threat called in at 3:30 a.m. cleared the building. As of this time, no casualties or injuries are reported. An organization calling itself *HDT* is claiming responsibility for the attack. Security footage shows four individuals placing the bombs at 3:00 a.m. Body recognition experts are able to identify three of the four attackers as Teddy Reed, Nassis Ball, and Effie Lee. The fourth attacker cannot be identified at this moment."

Images of Teddy, Nassis, and Effie went up on Screen one at a time, accompanied by biographical data. The package rolled over to a story about a pie-eating contest. RIFF23 paused it just as a man spread his mouth wide to insert a forkful of pie.

"That was her," Ronnie said.

RIFF23 removed the freeze frame, returning his Screen to black. Ronnie and Gret's faces looked back at them: reflected, distorted.

"The fourth person?" Gret asked.

"The fourth person," he confirmed. He saw it in her arms, the way she kept them close to her body, crossing and uncrossing them, sticking her hands in her pockets, zipping and unzipping her hoody. He watched her fidgety body, the body he knew, topped with a ski mask, looking back and forth as other ski-masked bodies planted contraptions around the lobby of a building. She played her part. She helped. She blew up a building.

They moved farther away from Doper's Memory and the roads became more substantial–the dust left stuck to the CAR. Strips of payday loan stores and nail salons replaced the field of dirt with its lone prairie dog.

The world stayed still and Ronnie moved past it in his glassed-in bubble. Some woman was in one of those shops selling her wedding ring and Hil was somewhere else blowing up buildings. Ronnie and Colin and Gret and RIFF23 moved down an uninteresting street toward home and Hil wore a ski mask and played look out.

"RIFF23?"

"Yes."

"Can you replay the footage?"

RIFF23 scanned through the entertainment package until he arrived at the news story about HDT. Gret and Ronnie leaned in again. Colin continued to sleep, his breath fogging up the window. They watched the stunned face of the news reporter as she adjusted her earpiece and squinted to read the teleprompter, and then the grainy black and white footage. Two ski-masked individuals walked in through a door in a dark parking garage. Two others stood outside the door, light on their feet, bobbing their heads around, checking for trouble.

"Pause it," Ronnie said.

The Screen froze.

"Zoom in on her."

She came closer. Her hands clenched at her sides in inept fists. The eyes that shown through the slit in the ski mask weren't hers, weren't anybody's, just black pools blurred and recorded.

The footage cut out, replaced by an image of a green telephone jumping around.

"Unknown number," RIFF23 said.

"Answer," Ronnie replied, shrugging.

No one appeared on the Screen, which showed a cartoon person–faceless and legless.

"Ronnie?" It was Laura Mills. RIFF23's speaker crackled.

Colin jumped, bumping his head against the window. "What the..." he started, but Gret shushed him.

"Hi, Laura," Ronnie said.

"Ronnie!" Bill's voice was even louder.

"You don't have to yell. I can hear you."

"Ronnie." It was Laura again. "Did you see?"

"How did you see?"

"Someone showed us."

"Who? They knew it was her?"

"We had someone..." Bill started. "When you told us about the studio, we had someone watching HDT, to figure out if she was really there. They brought us that story. We could tell right away, of course."

"The arms."

"Yes," it was Laura, now. For a few seconds no one said anything.

"What... the person who is helping you... what do they know?"

"That's actually why we called, Ronald," Bill said. "They found out some useful information, but we need someone to act on it."

FIFTEEN

Bill and Laura had no use for Ronnie. Hil loved him and that they understood. Were they not young intellectuals once, prime candidates for ill-conceived pairings? Laura spent an entire year of her life–19 years old, as beautiful as she'd ever be–dating a middle-school-educated drug dealer who wrote terrible poems.

"He looked like James Dean, though," Laura had pointed out.

"He wore a studded belt," Bill reminded her.

No, they didn't "get it," as parents hardly ever did, but he could be worse.

"He could be better, too," Bill was sure to mention.

After he made them aware of Hil's disappearance, they took it for granted that the entire thing was his fault and that he would be no help in finding her. They knew a guy. It wasn't that they were expecting their daughter to be kidnapped, but it was *to be* expected, so they had a guy. The guy's name might have been Lou or something equally stereotypical of a private investigator. Laura called him Lou when discussing things with Bill–"Lou called. He said he has a hot tip, or something." Bill called him Jim, and when in an inappropriately good mood, considering the circumstances, Inspector Gadget.

They didn't know his name. A friend of similar economic means referred him to them as "a guy who gets things done."

"Is he a hit man?" Laura whispered.

The friend looked at her disapprovingly and Bill chuckled.

Later, she asked, "Did he look at me like that because he isn't a hit man or because I wasn't supposed to ask?"

They never met Lou. He left notes on their doorstep. Sometimes the notes would tell them to be at the phone at a certain time. An actual telephone booth sat on the backside of their property, a brisk five-minute walk from the house. They usually walked out there twenty minutes before the appointed time, squeezed into the booth and waited. They were often silent, but sometimes one of them would point out a squirrel in a tree or a hummingbird at the feeder.

Jim was succinct.

"This HDT lead's pretty good," he said, and they started to wonder why they were paying him so much if he was impressed by a lead that came from Ronnie.

Eventually, Inspector Gadget proved his worth. "I found her," he said, before Laura could get in a "Hello."

He didn't have her, didn't know how to get to her, but he had proof that she was with HDT.

"What sort of proof?" Bill wanted to know.

It was aerial footage of the HDT compound. "Inspector Gadget was actually pretty good," Bill congratulated himself to Laura that evening. Lou bought a drone and flew it over the compound for a few hours and at some point he picked up a skinny, average height, brown-headed young woman who—at the time the drone passed over—walked through a patch of grass between various low-lying buildings, flanked by two people who were not physically forcing her to walk any particular way but seemed to be mentally willing her. Someone shot down the drone.

"Well, let's go get her," Laura said.

"Not easy," Lou said.

"And why's that?"

"They got bombs."

Bill grabbed the phone and yelled into it "Well call the fucking police then."

"Tried."

Lou did try. The police told him they were "assessing the situation," and suggested he avoid "proximity to the area or further drone activity."

Laura mentioned that she didn't really give a shit what they suggested.

Lou explained. There was no way in. The police told him this. They mentioned it as an unfortunate fact. He asked if they were trying to find a way in. They shuffled their feet around, muttered something about people always thinking things were easier than they really were.

So it was dangerous. There were booby traps, teenagers with guns, rumors of lookouts with bows and arrows up in the trees. Lou mentioned to the police that this was a terrorist organization they were dealing with. They just said they were on it and went back to their Screens, sighing in ways that were meant to let him know he was causing annoyance.

"We're on our own," Lou said helpfully.

One night the phone rang. No note from Lou came before. There was no telling how long it rang.

Laura couldn't sleep. She had an endless, irritating dream where Hil popped up and disappeared over and over again. First she sat in the living room and Hil sat beside her, leaning back on a cushion and eating apple slices. Laura turned her head away suddenly. She wasn't sure why. It might have been to call Bill. Maybe it was unbearable, looking at her missing daughter. When she looked back, Hil was gone. Then Laura rocked on the back porch. Hil rocked beside her.

"Anyway," she said, "if you want to find me..."

"Of course I want to find you!" Laura interrupted.

Hil shrugged.

They were on the beach–the water gray with pulped paper and tangled plastic forming a line between the sand and tide.

"So that's how," Hil said. She wore a white bonnet like they put on her head when she was a chubby, fair baby.

"What is?" Laura asked. She asked it casually, like the answer didn't really matter. She picked up a soggy cardboard disc that looked like something stuffed inside some useless kitchen utensil or toy to make it look presentable on the shelf in its shiny clear box, and flipped it into the ocean.

Laura was in bed and Hil stood over her. Laura tried to move but she couldn't. Her eyes were wide and she tried to smile at Hil, tried to say "Well hello stranger," but nothing came out. Hil leaned forward and whispered, "Pay attention, Mom."

She woke up gasping. Bill slept like a classy lady in a movie with a sleep mask and earplugs. He didn't react. Laura tapped him on the shoulder a few times, but he shrugged and rolled over.

Outside was dry and hot and silent in a way that made her wonder if she escaped the dream or was trapped under her covers. She wore one of Bill's t-shirts, slipping off one shoulder, advertising a marathon of which he was a sponsor but not a participant. As she moved down the path behind the house she felt an inevitable motion, like she was the forward swing of a pendulum, pushing her along. It was instinct, the distant faint ring directing her, though it was muffled out in the woods. When it became clear, when she knew "That is the sound of my phone ringing," she didn't rush. She walked along the path at the same pace and she answered in her calm voice: "Mills residence."

"You Laura?" the voice asked. It wasn't Lou. It wasn't one of Laura's girlfriends, drunk and up late. It wasn't Hil. The voice was young, didn't match the tough tone that a refusal to put all the necessary words in a sentence indicated. It was a girl's. She sounded like a teenager, like talking to an adult made her nervous and annoyed at the same time.

"Yes," Laura said.

"I'm with your daughter."

Laura breathed in deeply. Blew it out. Said: "Let me talk to her."

"No... like... I'm not with her right now, but I'm with her, you know?"

"At Walden?"

"Yes ma'am."

The girl breathed into the phone and Laura tried to listen behind her, to what the air sounded like where Hil was.

"Listen, ma'am," The girl sighed as if she'd put up with enough of Laura's nonsense. "Things are getting bad here. We're about to get real."

"What does that mean, honey?"

Maybe the girl liked being called honey. Maybe she had a mother somewhere who called her that. Her voice softened. "I think he's gonna make us... I think things are going to be public. Like online and stuff."

"What's going to be online?"

"The stuff we do."

"And?"

"And the people."

"How can I? How do I get her?"

"Look, I don't have a lot of time. Just look out is what I'm saying. I'll call back if I can. You've got to... You can't get her here. You've got to get her out there somewhere."

The phone clicked and the girl was gone. The sounds in the phone booth were just Laura's sounds.

SIXTEEN

Ronnie's entertainment subscription was up to fifteen packages. RIFF23 interrupted every meal and most conversations to alert him. The fact of a terrorist organization dominating the news cycle did nothing to offset the balance of entertainment offered. There were still cuddling animals and drunken revelry and bloggers fighting, and somewhere in the middle there were masked people planting bombs or sneaking into server rooms and leaking company documents.

Before the Internet Movies bombing, the initials HDT invoked a group of dirty old-timers who didn't believe in pesticides. Once the footage leaked, HDT became a social force–a confused tangle of revolutionary cultural icons and dangerous criminals.

All of a sudden they had a Profile, the only image one of Henry David Thoreau: chin-bearded, bow-tied, his hair flipping up in a little curl on top of his head. His eyes and mouth betrayed a pleased amusement at the proceedings of modern life.

"I don't know anything about that guy, but he looks like an asshole," Gret said.

Their profile said—the newscasters warned that some robot viewers may find the following quote upsetting—"Wake up, America! It's time to lay waste to the technology that controls you."

They made lovely stylized quotes over backgrounds of maroon mountains and bright blue oceans: "How near to good is what is *wild!*" "I believe in the forest."

People loved it. "Y'all are seriously like, my heroes," one commenter said.

"Keep fighting the good fight! I'd be there if I could," said another.

The newscasters interviewed some people. Did they really think it was OK what HDT was doing? "Yeah, man," a woman with a tilted beret told the camera, "They're pretty cool, I think."

HDT broke into the home of the CEO of FUN. They stole her jewelry and Screen. They spray-painted on the front door in red: "Sheep."

Amazon started selling t-shirts with Thoreau's face on them. His eyes twinkled atop 100% organic cotton.

In the footage, an unidentified body continued to lurk. The reporters guessed that he or she wore special padding to distort the shape of his or her body. Ronnie looked at the restless arms, the scrawny legs, the head that bobbed back and forth, playing lookout, and he wanted to punch something.

HDT started to play a game. They gave hints on their Profile about where they would go next. They asked for suggestions from the fans. They spotlighted their members.

"Losi West. Some know her as the sad orphan whose parents were locked up because they got in the way of THE MAN. Sad orphan no more, she's our fearless leader. Losi knows exactly what happens when real human life gets in the way of the technological elite, and she's tired of it."

The description was partnered with a picture of Losi, different from any that they found in Colin's files. She looked thinner. She stared, straight-mouthed at the camera, her head shaved, eyes sunken. She took up most of the frame, but just over her shoulder could be seen a patch of dirt, a dingy white piece of fabric, maybe a sheet out on the line to dry.

At 2:15 a.m. Ronnie's Screen started making a tinkling sound, followed by RIFF23 who rammed at the door and called "Alert! Alert!"

It was not an inspirational message over a lush background or a quiz called "Who's more evil: Hitler or RIFF bots?" It was another member profile.

"Here she is. The unidentifiable wonder. She's the daughter of the devolution, leading the revolution. She's been called 'heiress,' 'princess,' and 'trend-setter,' but we call her 'icon,' 'legend,' and 'queen.' Without her we would be nowhere. She brings zen to our compound and the truth to our hearts. Guess who."

The accompanying picture was a head in a balaclava, the eyes closed. The head rested against a wall made of wooden planks, splintering and pocked.

#

They weren't underground anymore. They were breaking news.

"Our guy says they're trying to be," Bill said.

It was four in the morning. They sat in the Mills' living room, drinking tea that Colin mentioned was "pretty good. Tastes like hot soy sauce."

RIFF23 rolled around taking it all in, Bill giving him a tour of the rooms. "It really is a lovely home!" he said. His Screen showed a thumbs-up. It was the first time he was allowed in, due to "special circumstances," meaning the Mills wanted to watch the news.

Ronnie sipped quietly from the salty tea. Laura was out at the payphone. Gret slept on a cushion. Colin ate carrots and rapped his fingers on the table.

"It was her!" Laura shouted, running in the door, the dark, hot morning, spitting her back into the lit house.

"Hil?" Ronnie, Bill, and RIFF23 asked.

She deflated, leaned against the doorjamb. "No... the other... the girl. The one from before."

Laura went over to Bill, who was in the corner with RIFF23 showing him a Walkman. He pressed a hand on her shoulder. "What did she say?"

"Those idiots that leave comments..."

"Trolls," RIFF23 informed her.

"They've been calling for an attack on VS. She says it's a big job. She says only a few of them get to go and Hil is one."

"Where?" Ronnie asked. He did not ask it like he should. He did not jump up and demand the information. He rubbed his eyes. He sighed. He had little hope. "Where are they going?"

"VS headquarters," Laura answered.

"South Korea," Gret informed them.

SEVENTEEN

"Please calm down, Hil," Effie said.

"Why should I?" I heard in my muffled voice the fear I was trying to hide.

"Because the same thing is going to happen to you whether you are calm or not, but I am going to be more stressed out if you aren't calm, and there's really no reason to make me feel stressed out."

"Why do I care about your stress?" I asked.

She slapped me in the face, the sound of it softened by the cloth sack over my head.

"I guess that's why," I said.

"Why don't you shut up?" she asked.

I shrugged.

Ronnie made me watch a lot of movies that involved tough, cool guys getting tortured and beat up, and they were always quippy. I never thought I would be in the same place as those adventurous film heroes, but if I had thought about it, I would have hoped to remain obnoxiously light-hearted during torture just like them.

I was doing my best, but it got harder each day. There were many things that went into getting held against your will–being verbally abused, partially starved, and sometimes beat up–that made it difficult to find the will to joke. However, I'd soldiered through so far, feeding off the amount of annoyance it caused my keepers. When I didn't have a bag over my head, I could see that they braced themselves when I opened my mouth. If I even started talking in a certain tone of voice, they knew I was going to make some sarcastic remark to which they'd have to respond in some hardass way, because they weren't funny. They were funny when they got mad, though.

"When you get mad, you lose," my mom used to say. It was such a dumb, mom thing to say that it took me a long time to realize it was true.

I had a hard time maintaining my Bruce Willis stylings with the bag over my head. I'm claustrophobic, and the feeling of my breath bouncing against the bag and back into my nostrils, distracted me, making it harder to come up with ways to piss Effie off. She was the most fun to piss off.

"We're supposed to be friends, Hil," she said. She was tying my feet to a chair. Next she would tie my arms behind my back.

"Effie. You are tying me to a chair. Well, to be fair, I never asked you if you were into the S&M scene, so maybe you think this is what friends do."

Since I couldn't see her, I was only able to envision how mad she was getting by the way she tugged at the rope and how her breath changed, becoming more labored, less regular, louder.

"Hil, we both want to change the world. I'm just trying to get you to work with me so we can do that together. As a team. All of HDT, we think you're great. We think you have so many great ideas. And we feel so lucky to have you here. If you would just cooperate, it would all be so much easier." She sighed. "I know you'll see it my way eventually, and knowing that gets me through each day."

"So if you knew that I wasn't going to see it your way eventually, you couldn't make it through the day?"

She started on my hands. "Well, I don't think of it that way."

"It's a pretty obvious way to think about it. It's basic logic. Don't they teach you logic in terrorism school?"

"I didn't go to school," she said quietly.

This was likely a classic Stockholm Syndrome type move, but it worked. I felt bad. A lot of the HDTers were tent people, uneducated and poor, HDT gave them something they lacked in their lives: a purpose, a place to fit in, not to mention food and shelter. It almost would be better for Effie to die than for her to turn against HDT, so empty would her life be without it. It was that very emptiness, that very preference for death, that made Effie and people like her excellent terrorists.

My pity for her gave way to the discomfort of the bag sticking to the moisture on my lips.

"If me deciding to be on your side is all that gets you through the day, Effie, I think you should stop getting through your day."

She paused, mid knot. "What do you mean?"

"Kill yourself."

Not so quippy after all. I could tell it wasn't a good one, since she didn't seem to get angry. She was probably sad, since she thought I was some sort of great beacon of light sent to lead the way, she the lamp meant to hold me, but she kept on tying her knots.

"Alright, Hil, you ready?" she asked.

I said nothing. I was too tired for a joke, too angry. Plus what did it matter if a person tied to a chair with a bag over her head was ready for the camera?

"Action!" Effie called. Someone, likely one of the younger boys who helped with media–I could never tell them apart, they were all dirty with shaved heads and scared eyes–hit a light that burned my eyes through the bag. I closed them.

"Here she is!" Effie proclaimed. "Our daughter of the devolution, here to lead a revolution! 'Why is she bound?' you might ask."

These parts always made me cringe. Johns wrote very flowery speeches for the poor girl. She could read, but not very well, and she never seemed to understand what to emphasize or when to rest. She didn't have the major downfall of most poor readers, though, which was the tendency to slip into a tired, stilted monotone. She remained enthusiastic, at an insane fervor, throughout the speech.

"She is bound to represent the metaphorical binds that bind us all! Fellow humans, we are nothing but prisoners to our Tech. Prisoners to our bots. Prisoners to our pictures. Our dear daughter will not stand for this. She cannot stand for this. She is bound to show you, dear, blind, humans, the ways in which you are constrained. Break free, dear humans, do not be deaf to the world around you, do not be deaf to our plea. Break free."

And then came the stupidest part: the big grand gesture. Effie approached me. I could feel her breath near my face. She cut my feet free first, then my hands. "Be free as she is free!" she yelled, and began to remove the bag, yelling, "Cut!" just before it rose above my chin. When she finally did remove the bag from my head, there were tears gleaming in her eyes. She smiled, proudly. "I think that was the best video I've done!" she said.

"Don't forget to give some credit to your leading actor," I pointed out.

"So true. You were great, Hil. You're always great!" She jutted her head out like a hen to kiss my cheek. I shoved her with my now free hands. One of the little shaved-headed boys grabbed me and started forcing me to walk away from her.

"I still love you, Hil!"

"The feeling is not mutual, Effie!" I called over my shoulder, as I was shoved out of the warehouse and into the intense daylight beaming into the forest. Johns was walking by with one of his lackeys, pointing at things in a self-important manner. He loved walking around like this, I assumed because he'd grown up watching his father walk around and point at things, but I'm pretty sure all he was saying was "Right there is a patch of grass, and look! The sky!"

"Hil!" he said, as if pleasantly surprised to see me here, in the place he was forcing me to live. "What a pleasant surprise."

I said nothing. Johns was just as sharp as me. Could match me joke for joke. What I found infuriated him the most was silence.

"Listen, Hil, we need to talk," he said, waving his lackey away and signaling to the kid who held me to let go. He took me by the arm and started guiding me toward my cell. "Hil, I know you're mad at me, but this simply won't do. We had an agreement, and you're not filling your end of it."

This was a trick he used sometimes, saying sort of vague things to try to force me to ask him questions. He really wanted me to talk to him. It was sort of sad, knowing the Johns I used to know, remembering how much he wanted everyone to like him. It was killing him to stand here with me and know that I hated him, that I couldn't even do him the common courtesy of exchanging words.

"Hil! You made a promise to me. You want to be a martyr for the people, right? You want to keep all those dopers and OTGers and babies and whoever else all over the world safe from Momma and Papa Mills' evil plan, right?"

Yes. He really talked like this. This was a man I used to possibly love, or at least found bearable enough to spend a large amount of time with. Was he always like this? Sometimes, secluded in my cell, hungry, angry, and out of things to think about, I closed my eyes and tried to remember Johns. I tried to remember the versions of Hil and Johns that existed before our current incarnation.

The summer we were 15, we tried to write a hit play. We both thought we were the misunderstood artists of our family, and we were also really into people who were in love and collaborated on projects. Saying we loved each other was not something we did, but we kissed sometimes and it was a thought that crossed my mind sometimes–not in the way of "I love him," more in the way of "Do I love him?"

The play was about two RIFF models who fall in love but their humans won't agree to let them go. It was about the moral ambiguities of artificial life, forbidden love, and the overlap between human and companion desires in the modern age. It was a terrible play. I kept a copy of it, and long after Johns and I broke up or whatever, even after we stopped seeing each other at all, I occasionally pulled it out and read it. To us, it was the funniest play that was ever written, because the whole play was full of our jokes. We would write two lines of dialogue and then start crying from laughter, take a break, make out a little, then come back and write two more. When we put the play on for our parents–Chele and Georgie filling the roles of the owners, while we were wrapped in tin foil to play the robots–the room was silent. Well, it was silent except for our lines and the "bleep blop bloop" noises we would make and the laughter we would break into, despite ourselves. During intermission Johns told me, "Think about something terrible! We have to stop laughing. You need to think about something really terrible and sad so you can stay serious." I couldn't come up with something. Finally he said, "Think about your mom dying." "What the fuck, Johns!" I said. "Well," he pointed out, "You're serious now."

Was Johns, wrapped in tinfoil, doubled over from some stupid line I'd written, still in there? Packed down deep inside the Johns who looked at me like he wished that he could own me? Or were their two different Johnses? The one who held my hair back the first time I puked from drinking too much and the one who walked around a terrorist compound pointing at the grass? Could both of those exist in one body, or did the new Johns have to kill the old one?

"Well? Hil?" I saw a glimmer of something I didn't like in his eyes.

"Yes, Johns, I want to keep everyone safe. I don't know if martyr is a great word, since I'm not really here all that willingly, but generally my answer is 'yes' to what you just said."

"It's nice to hear your voice," he said. His face softened. I could see a little bit of the old Johns there. "I hate when you don't talk to me." I considered responding to the dimming of the gleam and softening of his face by going straight back into silence, but decided it would be risky.

"Well, Johns, there's not much to say, is there?"

"Hil, I really thought you'd come around by now. You said you'd try. That was our agreement!"

"No, Johns. Our 'agreement'—which is really a generous word to use since it implies two parties with equal power in making a decision and not one person with a compound who kidnaps another person—was that you took my parents' chip and if I escape you'll release it. Well, I'm here. I don't know how I would escape, but I'm not trying. I'm just eking out my days until you get a grip or you mess up your food formula and I die."

"Shut up, Hil. Like I would let you die."

"Sometimes I wish you would." As with Effie earlier, this was much less light-hearted and quippy than I liked to be, and it scared me when I realized it was true.

For a while I could watch the proceedings around me with a vague amusement, albeit discomfort due to my own poor physical condition. I tried to think of it all as a funny story I'd tell Ronnie one day. But each day brought nothing new. The only time I was pulled from my normal routine of sitting in a cell, getting walked to the bathroom, getting walked around the grounds, and sometimes getting sat in front of the camera, were for fieldtrips–Do Bad Trips I called them–where I watched as HDTers blew stuff up or stole information. Things were bleak, and with each day, the big, expansive window through which I would one day make my great escape grew narrower and narrower.

The only not terrible thing around me was Losi. She would sometimes come and visit. It was hard with her, though, because I blamed her somewhat for what had happened. It wasn't actually her fault. I knew that she was just a means Johns used to try to get me to come to HDT willingly, which he quickly discarded when he saw it wouldn't work, but I still felt like if I'd never started writing her none of this would have happened. Plus, she founded HDT in the first place, and if she hadn't started her totally normal, nice, community, an insane person like Johns never could have come in and wrecked it. She was basically a prisoner herself, although she was less willing than me to show her true feelings, so they let her roam free on the compound as a figurehead. She wasn't allowed in any meetings or on any DBTs; she was just the wandering woman they believed had given them her blessing to ruin the world.

When I saw her approaching, my stomach instantly rumbled. She brought me peanut butter and apples and little packets of granola, which I scarfed down like an animal. She patted my head through the bars and I nuzzled against her touch like a dog. It was strange how I could see myself doing these things, could tell that they were strange and sad, but couldn't stop. I was split in two like Johns. I was the old Hil who could make a sarcastic remark about the most dire situation, and I was sad, lonely, beaten up, abused Hil who wanted to nuzzle the person who fed her.

"I think you're remembering our agreement wrong," Johns said. "And since, as you pointed out, I'm the one with all the power, I get to decide which one of us is right about the agreement."

"You know, you do a good job here," I said. I paused just long enough for him to think I was actually about to say something nice, before continuing. "Your torture is by the book. You don't feed me enough, I'm bored all the time and just when I stop being bored something scary and terrible happens, I'm dirty, I'm ugly, I have no one to talk to. But honestly, you could skip all of that and just torture people by making them listen to you talk."

He slapped me. Getting a slap from Johns was like getting an A+ on an annoyance test. He tried so hard to play good cop, to play master of his emotions, that it took a truly sharp dig to make him snap.

"Listen, Hil. I know more than you think I know," he said after we walked in silence for a few steps. I could feel him shaking where he held my arm. "I know all about your boyfriend. I know where to find him. You know I know where to find your parents. And like you said, you're stuck here, you can't leave, so you can't do anything about anything I want to do. You can't stop me. I'm only letting you have the illusion of power."

"Yes I feel very powerful," I said. I was still rubbing my cheek where it burned. He was right though, I somehow believed that by accepting my fate, by doing nothing more than talking back to my captors, and generally going along with whatever they wanted, I was keeping other people safe, that I was keeping Johns from using the data on the chip or hurting my family or hurting Ronnie. But really Johns could do any of those things any time he wanted, and I couldn't stop him or punish him. Which begged the question: why have me here at all? I guess if I was on the outside, and he'd stolen my data, I could be alerting others to what had happened and trying to gang up to stop him. That didn't seem like a creditable threat, though. I was well-liked, sure, and I didn't give up easily, but I wasn't nearly as powerful as Johns and even picturing my sad, little pacifist army made me laugh.

No, the real reason I was at HDT had something to do with my physicality. Even if I was there against my will, if I tried very hard to make it apparent to each person there that I hated them and what they stood for, me being there meant something. I think it mostly meant that they were powerful enough to exact power over someone like me, someone they'd all heard about, someone related in their heads to that evil word "Tech."

"So what do you want?" I asked, realizing that was what he wanted me to ask and that the conversation was going to be interminable if I didn't lead it down the right path.

"I want you to be more enthusiastic."

"How so?"

"First of all, it would be nice if we didn't have to do this whole tied to the chair schtick, if you would actually stand up and say some stuff."

"You want my face on camera?"

"No no. I know how you feel about that, Hil." He stroked my cheek where he'd slapped me. "I don't want to do that to you. We'd leave your face covered. We'd even distort your voice, but we want it obvious that it's you or someone like you under there, that that's why we're covering your face and distorting your voice."

"If it could just be someone like me, why don't you use Effie? She's about the same size as me."

"Hil, our followers pay close attention. Effie isn't you. They'll be able to tell the difference. We need the same body."

"Whatever."

"Is that a yes?"

"I have my own demands."

"Hil, you don't get demands."

We walked in silence back to my cell. When we got there, he shoved me inside, grunted a goodbye, and left.

# #

Losi came to me that night with a box of raisins and a pouch of applesauce.

She sat in the dirt outside my cell and passed them to me. I ate quickly. She waited. "Thank you," I said when I was done.

"Please don't thank me for giving you something you should have," she said. This was always the exchange.

"So how are you?" she asked.

I started to cry. Yesterday I would have said, "Oh, you know, got slapped twice today, so not too bad." Today I was actually thinking about how I was. Losi often seemed uncomfortable around me, squirmy, so I expected her normal awkward face to be peering back at me when I wiped away the tears, but she looked the most normal I'd ever seen her. I realized it might have been my lightheartedness that made her uncomfortable, if she was less delusional than me, she would have known all along that none of this was funny.

"None of this is funny," I sniffled.

She shook her head. "No. It isn't."

"Can we get out of here, Losi?"

"What about Johns?" she asked. "I mean, no, we can't. There's no way I know of. But even if we could, what about Johns and your data? I mean, I guess I might as well have tried a long time ago. I have no one I love to worry about. I just value my own life too much, I'm too afraid to die. I'd rather just be a lazy coward and wander around here until I get old and wither away."

"So we stop Johns. It's all just Johns, anyway. Not that I don't think he's capable of it, but I think the killing people I love thing is all talk. He wants me to like him, weirdly enough. It's mostly the data. I think he thinks I could still like him if he used the chip. Which means he doesn't know me."

"We're going to steal the data? You and me? The most incarcerated and the least trusted individual on the compound are going to combine our power and wits?"

"So much power," I said. "For example, I can sometimes stand up for at least a minute without getting dizzy."

She looked uncomfortable again.

"I'm realizing I'm probably just going to die here, and I might as well, because why live in a world where someone like Johns can run around and do whatever he wants?" I felt like crying more, but I was too tired.

"There are a couple of people I'm starting to trust here," she said. "The way they talk to me, the way they look at you, I can tell they know things here aren't OK. I want to be careful, but I think we can try getting some more people on our side."

"Be really careful, though. I said that thing about Johns not really wanting to kill my family or Ronnie, but that was mostly to make myself feel better. I have no idea what he would do."

"I'll be careful."

I stuck my head toward the bars for her to rub it for a few seconds, before some woman with a pink Mohawk and combat boots walked by and yelled, "Get a room!"

"Cool hair!" I replied.

EIGHTEEN

RIFF23 shouldn't have been able to get jet lag, but he somehow managed it. They were staying in a four-bunk room in a hostel. Gret insisted they all get in bed promptly at 10:00, because they had important things to do and didn't have time for sleep deprivation. Colin and Ronnie agreed. Ronnie assumed that they were all three lying on their backs, staring at the ceiling, praying for sleep. He was thinking of what he could think about to make him tired, and had come up with trying for the 100th time in his life to count sheep, which never worked, but usually did numb his mind in a way that segued into other weird thoughts that eventually became semi-dreams, and a half-wakeful state was better than a full wakeful one, especially when one needed to wake up in the morning and intercept a terrorist organization.

Ronnie's brain was just switching from sheep number 37 to a conversation with a man he'd never seen before about why that man's lucky number was 37, "Well, I have 37 kids, you see," the man was saying, when RIFF23 started moving around the room blasting some new pop song. "I know what you mean, girl put down your Screen!" he sang in his monotone voice. Three pillows flew at his lit up, rolling body, and he powered down.

The next morning, running on a combined four hours of sleep–except RIFF23 who was well-rested and peppy–the four took a bus to Sokcho.

# #

Sokcho was located on the northeast coast of South Korea, just south of the border with North Korea. Gret explained, that early morning at the Mills, that VS Headquarters were housed there, inside Seoraksan, a mountain surrounded by a park and Buddhist temple.

According to Laura's HDT Informant, the attack would happen in two days. "Go to the Buddha," she said.

# #

"What do we do if we see Johns or someone else from HDT?" Ronnie asked. "They'll recognize us and it will all be over!"

"On the bus?" Gret asked. "Ronnie, there is no way Johns is taking a bus. Do you even know about rich people?"

"Buses are slow," Colin whined. "Why do these even exist anymore?"

"For poor people like us," Gret pointed out.

"But couldn't we have rented a CAR?" Colin asked.

"We're poor!" Gret snapped. "So no. Unless you want to spend all the money we brought for food and shelter on getting somewhere faster..."

"But it's going to take five hours. I've never spent five hours getting anywhere in my life."

"You just spent 13 hours getting to this country."

"You know what I mean."

"No. I don't."

Colin, in the window seat, was leaning over Ronnie to talk to Gret in the seat across the aisle.

"I could switch with one of you," Ronnie said.

"We're fine," Gret said, crossing her arms and turning toward RIFF23.

"Yeah. Fine," Colin said, looking sadly out the window.

The bus dumped them in front of a G-Mart in Sokcho. "OK, that was pretty bad... and long," Gret said, looking at Colin. He refused to acknowledge she'd said anything.

"I'm starving," Ronnie said.

"That jelly rice thing the lady on the bus gave you didn't tide you over?" Colin asked.

They wandered around the streets looking for something to eat. They studied the pictures of food on the sides of the buildings carefully.

"I smell sea," Gret said.

"Sea? Like water?" Ronnie asked.

"Yep. Like salty water!" Gret said.

"We forgot about the sea!" Colin said.

They began walking toward the breeze they were feeling. As they got closer to the water, stalls popped up selling dried squid and fruit. A man biked by with a bundle of seaweed in his basket. People were gathered around small, round tables with grills in the middle, watching shellfish squirm and die. When they reached the beach, they walked up and down for a while, glancing in the windows of restaurants with big tanks of seafood. They finally settled on a restaurant that had a sign translated into English: "Squid Sausage!"

"I don't know what squid sausage is," Ronnie said, "but I want it."

They walked inside. The Korean workers and customers stared and smiled when they entered. They carefully took their shoes off and moved up onto a platform with a low table. They sat on the floor around it. A RAS model came over to their table.

"Hello!" the robot said, cheerfully.

"Hi!" everyone said back, except RIFF23, who asked, "Who are you?"

"I'm RAS3004 with BTF," she said.

"BTF?" RIFF23 asked.

"Like many RIFF models, you prefer to ask questions rather than search for answers internally. I respect this. BTF stands for 'Bonus Translation Function.'"

"Great! Well, RAS3004, we would love some... What's the alcohol you drink in this country?" Gret asked.

"Well. I don't drink, of course," RAS3004 laughed awkwardly. RIFF23 played the rolling eyes emoji. "However, the humans here enjoy a drink called soju. We have it here in an unflavored form, but also in kiwi and watermelon."

"Watermelon!" Ronnie and Colin said, excitedly.

"Wonderful. Well I'll get that right out for you and be back shortly to take your order." She rolled away.

RIFF23 was playing his patented annoyed emoji: a smiley face with a tilted mouth.

"Why are you so sore, RIFF23?" Ronnie asked.

"Why is she acting like translation is a bonus function! Any robot can translate."

"You can't," Ronnie pointed out.

"Yeah, but, that's because I only have so much drive space. I had to drop all languages except English to make room for emoji updates!"

"OK, but if RAS3004 wasn't here, we'd be pointing and acting like idiots, now we get to order well and communicate in our language," Gret said.

"Exactly, and not interact with a single local person!"

"Why does it matter to you?" Ronnie asked.

"I get it," Colin said. "RIFF23 has robot pride. He doesn't want dumb old RAS3004 ruining his good name."

"You would get it," Ronnie said.

RAS3004 reappeared with three shot glasses and a bottle of watermelon soju.

"Would you like for me to read the menu to you?" she asked. They assented, and she read the entire three-page menu, while they started in on the soju. When she was done, Ronnie said, "Three orders of squid sausage, please."

"Is that all?" RAS3004 said, disappointed.

"What else should we get?" Gret asked.

"A sea cucumber? They're a local delicacy."

"Great!" Gret said. "Three sea cucumbers it is."

"Great!" RAS3004 said, and left.

"So... who's going to eat three sea cucumbers?" Colin asked.

"Don't be a baby, Colin," Gret said.

"Yeah! We'll hide them in our napkins," Ronnie said.

After three extra orders of squid sausage, three failed attempts to try a bite of a sea cucumber, which looked like a floppy, dead penis, and was the consistency that Ronnie imagined one would be, and four bottles of soju, they left RAS3004 and wandered down to the water. Colin and Ronnie sat in the sand, while Gret walked along the water's edge. RIFF23 moved along beside her, ranting about RAS3004.

"So. Tomorrow," Colin said.

"Tomorrow," Ronnie replied.

"We have no idea what we're doing."

"Nope."

"Are we going to like... get killed?"

"Are you ok with that?"

"With dying for your girlfriend that I've never met? Not at all."

"Well, just stay alive, my friend," Ronnie said, he put his arm around Colin's shoulder for a moment, before they both forgot they were drunk and felt awkward and squirmed apart.

All of a sudden, Ronnie grew very still. He sat up straight and looked behind him.

"What?" Colin asked. Ronnie shushed him. He stood up and squinted back toward the restaurant. The sun was almost gone, and all he could make out were two human shapes, but he heard a familiar voice.

"Ronnie... What?" Colin asked. Ronnie shushed him again, and moved away from the water, toward the restaurant. Colin followed. As they got closer to the streetlights, Ronnie ducked behind a garbage can and Colin followed suit.

"Ronnie! You're shaking!" Colin whispered.

Ronnie nodded, but didn't say anything, just fixed his eyes on the street.

"Wait!" Colin hissed, "That's that Johns guy! Who's he..."

"That's Hil," Ronnie said finally.

"Well, dude, should we go..."

"I don't know! This wasn't part of the plan! I have to think!"

Hil and Johns walked a few steps closer to the trash can. Ronnie couldn't hear what she said, could only make out the familiar cadence of her voice, watch as her body moved–now anxiously standing on tiptoes, now crossing her arms, relaxing back on the balls of her feet. How strange to be a spectator to her, for her voice and shape to have nothing to do with him, to remember her as he once knew her–a body dancing at a party, a person he did not know.

Johns stepped toward her. He pointed a finger at his cheek. She kissed it.

They went inside the restaurant and Ronnie ran down to the edge of the water, bent over, and dry heaved. Colin hung back for a few seconds. When Ronnie stood up, he approached slowly. "You OK, dude?" he asked. Ronnie just looked at him. "So what should we do now?" Colin asked. Ronnie shrugged and sat down in the sand.

Gret and RIFF23 joined them.

"Where were you?" Gret asked.

"We found Hil," Colin said.

RIFF23's Screen erupted into a grinning emoji. He looked around and asked, "Well where is she?"

"With her boyfriend," Ronnie said.

"Huh? What did she say to you?" Gret asked.

"Well we never actually talked to her..." Colin said.

"What do you mean you didn't talk to her?" RIFF23 asked. "Where is she? What is wrong with you?"

"She's at the squid sausage place," Ronnie said, "with, as I already said, her boyfriend."

"Stop acting like a teenager and explain what you mean," Gret said.

"She was with Johns," Colin said.

"I feel like we've been over this," Gret said.

"We have," Colin replied.

"Great! Ronnie, we've been over this. Johns isn't Hil's boyfriend, you're crazy to think that. Now let's continue with the plan."

"She kissed him," Ronnie said, quietly.

"Man, yeah. But it was on the cheek?" Colin said, unsure.

"Look. We don't know what's going on with Hil one way or the other. If Johns is her boyfriend. I mean whatever. We're here. We need to at least try to rescue her if that's what she wants," Gret said.

"And if that isn't what she wants?" Ronnie asked.

"Then I guess she's the enemy and we fight against her as well," Gret said.

"Wait! Who said anything about fighting 'the enemy'?" Colin asked. "I thought we were just saving this chick and leaving!"

"So, you're OK with letting this terrorist organization just keep doing what they're doing? Blowing shit up?" she asked.

"Man, I don't know. Some of the stuff I like. Not all of it. Not the killing people part. But isn't that like, not our business?"

"Whose business is it, then?"

"I don't know. The authorities?"

"And have you seen the authorities doing anything about this?"

"Gret, I understand where you're coming from, but are you really suggesting that we exact vigilante justice?" Ronnie asked.

"Well. Yeah. That's what I assumed we were all planning on doing."

RIFF23 let out a long whistle.

"Listen. Whatever. If you guys don't want to help. Whatever. First thing's first, though. We need to talk to Hil. We need to figure out where she stands on all this."

"She stands next to her boyfriend, most likely," Ronnie said.

"Shut up. OK so let's think. She's in there. Johns is in there. We need to find out who else is in there. RIFF23, you're the most generic-looking of us, you go take a peek," Gret said.

"Gee thanks," RIFF23 said, moving toward the restaurant.

He came back a few minutes later and said it appeared to be only Johns and Hil.

"Like they're on a date?" Ronnie asked.

"Oh, Ronnie, will you..." Gret started.

"Yes." RIFF23 interrupted. "It looked very romantic. They were sharing a sea cucumber."

"OK! I have a plan," Gret said.

It was a very stupid plan, but as they'd been saying a lot lately, it was the only plan they had. First, RIFF23 would have to talk to RAS3004. "Nope. I quit this plan," he said. He would need to somehow convince RAS3004 to help them without actually giving her any information about what they were doing. "OK. Fine. I will let you in on a secret. Robots love human romance. OK, not all robots. I for one can't stand it. I think if we tell RAS3004 that Ronnie is in love with Hil and he's trying to win her back, she'll help us out."

"I don't want her back," Ronnie muttered. Everyone told Ronnie to shut up, and they decided to go with RIFF23's plan. The three humans waited on the beach while RIFF23 went around to the back of the restaurant and talked to RAS3004. He came back after only a few minutes. "I was right. She barely even wanted an explanation. She is all about this plan." Ronnie and RIFF23 were to meet her at a dumpster behind the restaurant in fifteen minutes. "Whatever," Ronnie said, lying down in the sand.

"Get up!" RIFF23 said. "You can't have sand all over you when you see Hil!"

"Why does it matter?" Ronnie asked. "This is pointless. It's probably worse than pointless. Probably when she sees me she's immediately going to call ole Johns over and he's going to kick my ass and then I'm going to get killed however terrorists kill people."

"Slowly," Colin said.

"Colin, you aren't helping," Gret said. "Ronnie. We don't know the full story of what's going on. Besides, you know Hil. Even if she is with Johns and is somehow into HDT, there's no way she's the kind of person who would just turn you over to be executed."

"'Executed,'" Ronnie said. "There you go. That's a very terrorist word for killing people."

"Ronnie, time is running out," RIFF23 said. "We need to go meet her."

"Why don't you go meet her? I'll wait here. Tell her I said 'sup?'"

Gret grabbed Ronnie's ear and yanked his head so that he was eye level with her. "Ronnie. You need to cut this out. Stop feeling sorry for yourself. No one is impressed. Get your shit together and go do what you need to do."

He followed RIFF23 begrudgingly. For a while his anger and sadness had covered up the underlying way he was feeling: nervous. He hadn't seen or talked to Hil in over two months. How would she look at him? What did he even look like? He stopped taking care of himself a while ago. He couldn't remember if he brushed his teeth that morning. RIFF23 was right! He shouldn't have gotten sand all over him. He probably looked like some bum off the streets. She might not even recognize him. He hoped, of course, that the things he'd been saying were untrue: that Hil was not with Johns, was not on the side of HDT, but he also feared they were. Gret was right, Hil wouldn't try to have him killed, unless she was a brainwashed zombie, but even so, the idea of her telling him to leave, that she didn't need his help and was happy where she was, scared him.

According to RIFF23's clock, they'd been waiting at the dumpster for twenty minutes, and still no Hil.

"Maybe RAS3004 couldn't come up with a good excuse to get her to come back here," Ronnie said.

"I told her to bring them free soju, and then whenever one of them got up to go to the bathroom she should make her move: either grab Hil from the table or grab her on the way to the ladies. So the fifteen minute thing was just an estimate."

"Lord, RIFF23. You know Hil has the world's strongest bladder."

"I sort of forgot about that. We'll just have to hope Johns is worse off."

"Wait... *free* soju? Who's paying for it?"

"I transferred her some funds."

"You mean my funds?"

The back door opened, and RAS3004 rolled out followed by Hil who was saying, "I'm sorry, but I don't get it. People from the States get a tour of what, exactly? Your trash?" She saw Ronnie and RIFF23 and stood very still. RAS3004 said, "You have five minutes, most likely. I put a little bit of laxative in the gentleman's food so he should be in the bathroom for a while." She rolled back inside and Hil continued to stay where she was, stalk still right outside the door.

"Ronnie," she said finally.

"Hil," he said.

There was a long silence, before RIFF23 finally said, "I know this is quite a moment, you two, but you have five minutes, so let's get down to it."

Hil ran over to Ronnie and squeezed him around the middle. He held her. She'd lost weight. He could feel her boniness beneath his arms. He breathed her in. After all these months, after whatever she'd been through and wherever she'd been, she smelled the same: like baby powder and sweat. He kissed the top of her head over and over again. He could feel her crying, the shuddering intensity of it, could hear the way she was choking down the sounds of her sobs. She kissed him. They pulled apart and looked at each other.

"You look terrible," she said.

"So do you."

"Listen," RIFF23 started, he was playing a crying emoji. "Listen. I'm sorry. I wish. But no. Listen. You have three minutes and 43 seconds left."

"Hil. How do we... What do you... Are you dating Johns?"

"What? No!"

"Do you want to be in HDT?"

"What the fuck, Ronnie? No!"

"How can we save you?"

"You're here to save me without a plan of how?"

"Our plan was to come here. That's as far as we got."

"The day after tomorrow, they're doing this attack..."

"On the VS servers. We know."

"I want to stop them. Losi and I. Losi is..."

"I know who she is."

"Well, we're trying to stop it. Then we want to get out. But it has to... It's not going to be easy."

"How close an eye do they have?"

"Very close. This five minute laxative thing is the first time I've been away from a member since they took me."

"So what do we..."

"Ronnie five minutes isn't enough time to explain. We have contacts on the outside. We have someone helping us. You need to find this guy Lin. He'll be at the Haslla café tomorrow at eleven a.m."

She kissed him, then RIFF23, and ran back inside.

NINETEEN

They spent the night on mats in a lofted area above a spa. The women and men had separate sleeping areas, cordoned off by a flimsy screen printed with bathing ladies that ran across the center of the loft. They were the only ones in the building, so Ronnie, Colin, and Gret all slept against the screen so they could whisper through it. RIFF23 was in a far off corner of the men's side, powered down and charging.

"We don't know what we're doing," Gret whispered.

Ronnie kept his breathing steady, his body straight, so that they might think he was asleep and he would not have to respond.

"We have Lin," Colin said, without much conviction.

Ronnie did not know if he slept. The night was an interminable intention to go to sleep, a desperation to fall away from himself. When the sun rose he thought he could have opened his eyes or they could have been open all along, and only remembering their function by the introduction of light.

He didn't feel like he had seen Hil, or he did not feel the way he thought he should after seeing her. There was no long-awaited relief, no end to the piling questions, only a sorrow amplified by the stabbing sun and the thin mat and Colin's snores.

#

Haslla Art World was a hotel and museum, according to RIFF23's research. A bus left the terminal outside of the spa every half hour for Haslla. They got on the 9:30 bus. The seats were full of happy couples in matching t-shirts, grandmothers with big visors, and parents with bouncing kids on their laps.

Ronnie led them to the empty back bench. He leaned his head against a window and allowed himself to be jostled, pretending he had no muscles to tense. The beaches passed him by while he stayed in one place. The trees and houses and businesses, stacked together as if they all grew at the same rate, were seeds planted at the same time, also moved by him.

When the world stopped moving, the bus driver called "Haslla!" The bus crouched and creaked as the door swung open and everyone got off. It was a brightly striped building, outlined in dulled steel. A statue of an overweight tourist in a Hawaiian shirt, clinging to his wife, greeted them at the entrance. They followed signs for the cafe.

It was a wide room with large windows looking out on the grounds: ocean, gardens, woods. A woman stood behind the bar, rubbing the same spot with a stained rag in a desultory manner. There appeared to be no one else in the room. The crowd from the bus had dispersed over the grounds.

Gret leaned anxiously on the bar, smiled at the woman who did not smile back. "We're looking for Lin," she said.

The woman threw the rag over her shoulder and walked off.

Gret looked at the others who shrugged.

"Maybe she doesn't speak English?" Colin said.

A man replaced the woman behind the bar and started rubbing the same spot, which Ronnie noticed was worn and dull, compared to the rest of the wood bar, which was brightly varnished.

There was a strange, 3D rectangle in the man's breast pocket. He reached his fingers in toward it and pulled out a cigarette, stuck it in his lips, and kept scrubbing.

"Um," Ronnie began, "excuse us. We were looking for someone named Lin."

The man patted his pants pockets and came up with a lighter. He lit the cigarette.

"I haven't seen anyone smoke in..." Ronnie started. "I've never seen anyone smoke!"

"That's bad for you, you know!" Colin added.

The man looked up at them, his eyes moving across each face, took a deep drag of the cigarette, and blew out a smoke ring.

"Maybe he doesn't speak English either," Gret said quietly.

"I'm Lin," he said.

"Oh. Well," Ronnie said, "Should we exchange some sort of password or something?"

Lin shrugged.

"OK. Um. Well Hil sent us here."

Lin nodded.

"Just. Real quick. Look. RIFF23 pull up some pictures of gross lungs or something!" Colin said.

Lin grabbed a shot glass from under the bar and stubbed the cigarette out in it.

The three humans across the bar from him coughed dramatically. RIFF23 played a picture of a cigarette with a slash through it.

"Let's walk," Lin said.

They made their way out of the building and down a gravel path through crumbling, large versions of the Venus of Willendorf, and some items that might have been art or litter or both. They came out into a field of bronze, human-sized severed thumbs.

"Great," RIFF23 said. "Art."

Lin sat on one of the thumbs, reached for another cigarette, changed his mind, and started jittering his leg.

"So," Ronnie started, deciding it would be up to him to get any information out of Lin, since he didn't seem interested in speaking first, "You work here?"

"No," Lin said.

"OK. Cool," Ronnie kicked some dirt and looked around at the others for help.

"You know Hil?" Gret asked.

"Of her."

RIFF23 broke out the volcano: "Listen here, buster! We need answers and we need them now!"

Lin went for the cigarettes, grabbed one, lit it quickly and took a long drag.

Colin plugged his nose and walked several steps away, tripping over a thumb.

"Damnit! Y'all are making me nervous!" Lin yelled. He spoke with a surprising southern drawl. He threw the cigarette on the grass and rubbed it into the dirt with the toe of his shoe.

"Littering!" Colin yelled. "Littering!"

RIFF23 extracted his pick up tool and gingerly grabbed the cigarette, stashing it in his trash compartment.

"Let's all just calm down," Gret said. She sat on a thumb, and motioned for the others to join her. Colin squeezed onto the thumb with her, and Lin and Ronnie took one opposite.

"We were told to find you," Ronnie said again, "by Hil. If you have any idea why, or any information for us, we would appreciate it."

"Y'all part of this plan?" Lin asked.

"We're not sure," Ronnie said. "Which plan do you mean?"

"The plan to stop the plan."

RIFF23 played an eye-rolling emoji.

"We need a little more information than that," Ronnie prompted.

"There's a plan to hack VS. There's another one, from what I gather, to stop the hack."

"Yeah. I guess we're part of that plan," Ronnie said. "We just don't know what it is."

"We'll get there, I suppose," Lin said sadly.

"What's your part in all this?" Gret asked.

"I work for VS," he said, simply.

They waited for more. It didn't come.

"So what, you work over there at the headquarters?" Ronnie asked.

Lin nodded.

"And do what?"

"Head of IT."

"So, VS knows about the attack, I guess. The rumors are out there, so now they're working on stopping it, and... you somehow got in touch with Hil?"

Lin shook his head. "None of that. Nope."

"Well? What then?"

"I've been following HDT for a while now. Thought it sounded nice at first. Working with Screens all day will do that to a person, make you turn hippie."

RIFF23 flashed a peace sign on his Screen.

"Had a friend back home, I told her about them. She went right over there. Told me she'd write me a letter sometime, that this was it for her and Tech. Seemed like a lot of time passed, a few months maybe, and I never got that letter, which was her choice, I guess, but then I started hearing strange stories about HDT, bombings and stuff."

One day he got an encrypted call. It was his friend.

"Shit's out of control over here," she said.

"Yeah, since when do you blow stuff up?" he wanted to know.

"Since never."

It wasn't what she expected, she told him. He felt a pang, more than a pang, really, of guilt, since he was the one who introduced the idea into her hippie head. She couldn't leave now. He wanted to know how she was calling him. She told him she snuck her Screen in through a false-bottom box filled with Library of America Thoreau books.

"You were already suspicious?"

"No I just didn't think I could live without it."

It wasn't easy, though, using the thing. She had three roommates. This was her first attempt. She was squatting off in the woods, she said, taking a solo hike, which was frowned upon but not explicitly against the rules.

"I had to get to you, though," she said. "It's VS."

# #

It was before the news coverage. Most people still didn't know anything about HDT. Lin went straight to Field. He told him there were rumors, that there was this OTG group making waves, that they might be targeting VS soon. Field nodded gravely, adjusted his Spike bobble-head doll, tapped notes into his Screen.

"Thank you for letting me know, Lin," he said.

They shook hands.

That afternoon, Lin got a message that his security clearance was downgraded. He went to the head of security, explained he had to have top security clearance to go to the department head meetings.

"Someone else will be going to those," the tired Security Chief told him.

"But I'm the department head!"

The Security Chief asked him to leave.

# #

When his friend called again to let him know the date of the attack, he tried to see Field again. He couldn't get on Field's floor anymore with his demoted security clearance, so he put in an official meeting request. It was denied.

He fired off a message about the attack and the date. Field wrote back swiftly, "Thanks so much for your concern and dedication to this company."

Field sent out a memo to all HQ staff informing them that headquarters would be closed for routine maintenance for a week that included the date of the attack. They would all receive paid leave for that week. Lin hoped that this was part of a defensive plan, that security would stay behind, the rest leave for their own protection, but when he asked someone in security if they had to work that week, they looked at him blankly and asked "What part of paid leave don't you understand? You think I'm going to get paid and stay?"

#

"Maybe they just want the building clear because they're worried there will be explosives," Ronnie said.

Lin shrugged. "Or maybe they're part of the plan."

"That would be good, right?" Gret asked.

"Not the plan to stop the plan, but the plan."

TWENTY

Besides feeding me and rubbing my head, Losi's visits usually involved a part of her story. The only thing I was given to do was read *Walden*, which was one of the most boring and idiotic things I'd ever read, but I read it any way.

"How are you into this?" I asked Losi. "How could you found a group based on this guy?" I thumbed through for one of the many lines I underlined in anger: "'Often the poor man is not so cold and hungry as he is dirty and ragged and gross. It is partly his taste, and not merely his misfortune. If you give him money, he will perhaps buy more rags with it.'"

"He had some good ideas."

"Someone tries to give him a door mat and he says 'It is best to avoid the beginnings of evil'!"

"Look, Hil," she said. "I was sad and lonely. I found some quotes that sounded smart, you know? And here we are."

"Johns loves it, though."

"Oh yeah he's got the quotes down."

Just the other day, I'd asked Johns if I could possibly be moved into a room instead of the stupid makeshift jail he made me with bamboo bars. He said, "Much it concerns a man, forsooth, how a few sticks are slanted over him or under him, and what colors are daubed upon his box."

Forsooth.

That part of Losi's life between finding quotes in a silly book written by a pompous man who–I read in the biographical information in the back of my book–once started a massive forest fire, and living on a full-fledged terrorist compound was the part I wanted to know about. Every time she visited, Losi would give me a little more of the story, and when she was away I would ponder it. I would imagine her all teenage-angst and childhood trauma and try to connect the dots from where she left off to the present, until she came back to do it for me.

Losi's story might be the only one in history where a solitary road trip turned into the founding of a terrorist organization.

She was a really sad kid. Her parents were in prison for life on some trumped up charges. Her adopted parents didn't seem to really care about her. She was shy and nervous and didn't know how to communicate with other people, so she came across rude and aloof and superior. She didn't have any friends. Her new parents gave her a companion bot, but because she didn't have any friends or family to set an example, she didn't know how to program her. She assumed the bot wouldn't really be interested in hanging out with her or dealing with her problems, so she just programmed her to be disinterested in whatever Losi did. As Losi got older, she grew angrier, and she programmed her bot accordingly.

Losi didn't have anyone in her life that she cared about. I guess she cared about her parents in a sort of remote way. She told me she missed them, but she didn't really know what she was missing, it was more that she wondered what it would be like if they were in her life, if she would feel differently, if she would love them and feel a part of their world and not be alone.

When she hit puberty, she became interested in punk music. Since she was alone all the time, she had lots of little pet interests that she would spend time researching. She obsessively read about types of spiders, solved and built difficult mazes, watched every 1960s Italian horror film, and read every book by and about Flannery O'Connor. Eventually she stumbled on punk and it became her world. Unlike her previous obsessions, it was a world in which she could see other people like her–angry people, isolated people, people who liked loud music–and with whom she thought she might actually enjoy spending time. She holed herself up in her room and read article after article, watched videos, turned up her music. She still didn't talk to anyone, but she thought about it. Sometimes her fingers would hover just off her Screen, and she would consider liking, sharing, saying something, but she never did. Well, she never did until she did.

She found out this band she loved was playing in a town nearby. For the first time in her life she felt excited about going somewhere besides her bedroom to research. She posted something on some forum about how she was going to be there. "I'm sure all the other punks there were like 'who are you? Why do we care?'" she told me.

It made me feel a weird little aching sadness to picture her in that moment: lonely sweet Losi, with her black clothes and her septum piercing and her shaved head. She was tiny and she never smiled and her eyes were large and serious. I wanted to cry, and sometimes did, thinking about this person I had grown to love finally feeling anticipation, excitement, looking forward to something good happening in her life.

So she went to the concert and it was sort of how she thought it would be and sort of not. She talked to a few people-nothing serious, just a few hellos and this band is great rights-and she felt a little like she belonged, but still a little self-conscious. There were moments where she was so absorbed by the music that she forgot where she was and she thought about nothing at all and she felt completely herself and completely at ease for the first time in her life. It was a good night for her.

She'd never left her town, or even her neighborhood or her house, really, except to go to school. Returning home, through the darkened windows of the CAR, she watched the earth pass-spots of green cropped up along the landscape, wilting plants propped up with wire, surrounded by intricate, timed watering systems, skinny Tent People, watching her, shading their eyes—framed by the repeating parabola of mountains in the distance. "Walden – 10 miles" a sign read.

"What is Walden?" she asked.

"Walden, known colloquially as Walden Pond, is actually a lake. Famously observed in the work *Walden; or, Life in the Woods* by Henry David Thoreau, 19th Century transcendentalist," the CAR answered.

"Re-route to Walden," she said.

The CAR obeyed. They rode the ten miles until they arrived at a smaller, wooden sign that simply said "Walden" with an arrow pointing toward a dirt road. As the trees around the road grew tighter around the CAR, her heart began to beat in her throat. She felt afraid, but she also felt happy, a happiness that dwarfed the pleasure she felt when listening to her loud music. When the path grew too narrow for the CAR to fit, she parked and started to walk. As she walked, she ran her hands along the bark of trees, knelt down to touch the cool dirt, smelled the long grass, and picked up sticks to poke at scurrying bugs. The woods opened back up, and she found herself staring at the lake. It was very still. She went to the edge of the water, sat down, took her shoes off, and dipped her toes in.

As important as that night would be for Losi as a developing human, or could have been if that was all there was to it, it ended up becoming a footnote to the larger history of the founding of HDT.

"And that was it, I guess," she told me. "I sat there feeling the happiest I'd ever felt. I was grinning like an idiot. I was listening to birds chirping, you know? I mean it was a whole cliché sort of experience and it was wonderful. So I sat there and I tried to figure out why I was so happy. It was like a painful level of happiness: a smile that hurt my face, my heart pounding against my chest. I think it was because I was alone... Or I thought it was because I was alone. Thoreau says, 'Not till we are lost, in other words, not till we have lost the world, do we begin to find ourselves...'

"Now, it's all muddled together with this other stuff, and I'm less stupid, but it still makes sense. I was alone. I spent a lot of my life alone–most of it, in fact–but I was always engaged in something: reading about some stupid topic, listening to music, watching videos, programming bots, watching watching watching, listening listening listening, reading reading reading.

"Sometimes... I mean now everything is awful, of course, and I hate it here, but the one thing that is still good is just that my eyes don't hurt and my brain is calm. You know what I mean? I guess you just had the limited interaction with Screens in the first place, but if you're like me, like most people, it's just your whole life and it is exhausting. When I was dipping my toes in the water there was nothing there except me and the woods and the water and I had left my Screen in the CAR so I couldn't even look up any facts about the place or take any photos or anything. I was just there.

"You think he's an idiot, I get it, but Thoreau also said 'We are all sculptors and painters, and our material is our own flesh and blood and bones,' and I like that idea. That was what I wanted. To make something of my life."

I sighed and pulled out the book again and read to her. I read the only thing I underlined because I liked it and not because I hated it: "I went to the woods because I wished to live deliberately, to front only the essential facts of life, and see if I could not learn what it had to teach, and not, when I came to die, discover that I had not lived. I did not wish to live what was not life..."

She looked at me like she was lost then, her eyes roaming my face, like she just remembered something terrible.

#

She didn't stay at the pond then. She took out her Screen and found the nearest antique store.

Entering Aunt Twickie's, hearing the tinkle of a real bell, smelling the must of old things, Losi felt something similar to what she felt when she entered the woods.

"Hello?" Losi called into the silent space.

A grey-haired woman, gripping a gold cane, followed by a Robots are Dogs (RAD) model, came out of a back room.

"How can I help you, sweetheart?" she asked, moving her hand along Losi's cheek, rubbing her fuzzy shaved head.

Losi shivered and shook the woman off.

"I'm looking for a book. *Walden*."

"Oh, yes. I have that of course." She turned down a hallway, her RAD making irritating panting noises and nudging her calves.

"Quit it, RAD002," she hissed. "I hate this damn thing. My son gave it to me so he doesn't have to visit. If he thinks this is the sort of thing I want, then I don't want him to visit anyway."

"Just get rid of it," Losi said.

The woman didn't respond.

They entered a narrow room filled with books. All four walls were lined with shelves, and books were stacked on the floor.

"Over there are some copies of *Walden*," the lady said, yawning, "Take a look around and come let me know when you're ready to check out."

Losi grabbed a random book off the floor, opened the pages, and inhaled.

When she emerged from the room, she found the woman asleep in a chair. She transferred the funds for the books to Aunt Twickie's account, grabbed RAD002, yanked out his wires before he could start barking, and exited.

When she returned home, Losi stopped going to school. She stayed home and read her book.

"You really should go to school," her new parents said to her once, trying to pretend to care before leaving for a month-long drum circle retreat.

She felt miserable, and the only thing that brought her happiness was the thought that she could take the CAR any time she wanted back to Walden. So one day she did just that.

The main thing I couldn't figure out was why Losi—a person who seemed to have no interest in ever being around any other people, and particularly felt at her peak happiness while alone with her toe dipped in some water—would want to tell anyone else about Walden. "Why didn't you just keep it to yourself?" I asked her.

"Strong, sudden emotions can sometimes change you, at least temporarily. They can make you do things you wouldn't normally do. Walden made me feel some sort of kindness to the world... It was like I had to share it. I wanted to share it. I all of the sudden loved everyone and wanted them to be happy too."

It didn't last long. Not that she started to suddenly hate everyone, but when the Tent People nearby noticed her poking about and came to talk to her, it was an adjustment. She wasn't sure how to be friendly to people, but she did her best. She started by making tea for everyone. They would sit and talk, mostly about the things they saw: pointing out leaves and birds and clouds. They would go on hikes together deep into the woods and gather berries. They shared some seeds with her and showed her how to garden. Eventually, she asked them to join her there on the water. Some agreed. Even though she wasn't alone anymore, she still felt happiness. Her happiness changed to a complicated form–she was frustrated sometimes, she got annoyed with people, she wanted to be left alone, she had her first fit of laughter, she cried because of something someone else was feeling, and she lay awake worried about the safety of her little group.

Then Johns came.

Losi thought that, at most, her little Dark Web video might inspire some people to go outside more. She didn't think anyone would actually show up at Walden. She was happy with her community and content to live out her days without many adjustments. When Johns came barreling up the dirt road in his CAR, everyone hid. He parked and came out whistling, looking around casually. He peeked into their tents, checked out some of the huts they were starting to build, and looked at his reflection in the still water. Finally, he yelled: "OK, I can hear all of you breathing, I'm not a murderer or anything."

"Prove it!" Losi yelled back.

"Well, I'm not killing anyone right now, am I?" he said.

She thought that was funny. The story of many people getting pulled into Johns' foolishness could be summed up by "she thought that was funny." She came down and convinced the others to do the same.

Johns introduced himself to everyone. They found him charming, of course–so handsome and polite. He told her that he just found her post on the Dark Web and decided to come right over.

"Just like that?" she asked.

"Just like that," he said.

And that was it for a while. Johns set up his own tent. He helped plant and build and he even had a banjo he brought with him and played around the fire at night. Things were nice. Then they weren't.

"I think all Tech should be dead," he said one night after dinner as they lay by the fire.

"Yeah. Same," Losi said sleepily.

"So, let's kill it then."

It started out innocently enough. At least, that's what Losi said, until I pointed out to her that it really wasn't that innocent. They started going to private homes and wiping the memory of all the bots in the house. Often, if they had time, they would dismantle them as well. Johns started spray painting "HDT" on the walls of homes. Losi claims she never did that, but I thought she might have just been too embarrassed to fess up. Johns liked being destructive for a while, but then he got bored. He said he wanted to make more of a statement. So he started targeting companies. He looked for small ones with weak security. He would remotely hack them and wipe their files.

Losi stopped joining him on his little adventures. He kept a Screen stashed just off the main road so that he wouldn't be violating any rules of Walden, but could still have resources to hack. When he would walk down the road to do his business, Losi found herself hoping he would somehow get lost and not return. She could sense everyone around her relax a little when they saw him retreating into the woods. They would talk a little freer, laugh a little more often. But Johns always came back. Then he brought his people.

She couldn't remember if it was the people or the prison first. Either way, at some point, more of the people at Walden were there for Johns, and everyone had less freedom. Johns set up guards at the road to deter any tourists (they never came, but the guards served just as well to deter any HDTers from exiting the premises). He formed a group of key advisers. Unsurprisingly, none of them were original HDT members. He started holding weekly mandatory meetings for all members where he would spout his thoughts on HDT's mission and talk about upcoming targets.

"I should have shut it all down immediately," Losi told me. "The minute I realized what Johns was up to, I should have left and encouraged everyone else to do the same. We could have started a new community somewhere else, not aligned with any political agenda. We wouldn't tell anyone where we were. We could have lived alone, and undisturbed. But I was happy here with my little hut and my garden and I had finally started to like people and I was surrounded by them, and I thought we could just ignore Johns, separate ourselves from him, and eventually he would go away. He went from a concern to a serious problem so quickly, by the time I realized I should do something, it was too late. I would put everyone in danger. I would put myself in danger. So I took the easy way out. I stayed in the little hut I love with some of the people I love, even though they are miserable. It's awful, but sometimes I still think I like it better than the life I had before."

TWENTY-ONE

In my dreams I swallowed the chip. I slid it onto my tongue, let the saliva build up, gulped. I found it on the ground while wandering in the woods, looked in the mirror and saw it nestled in my jugular notch, glanced down and it was in my hand. Once Johns held it out in front of me and I licked it out from between his fingers.

"You can't really do that, you know," Losi warned. "It could mess up your intestines."

Would it matter if I crushed it, burned it, swallowed it against Losi's advice? Johns may have copied it, probably did. It was just a symbol, but we had nothing else to grab.

Because it was something we could grab, he dangled it in front of us. Johns wore it around his neck in a leather pouch. Sometimes when he talked to me he took the pouch out from under his shirt and rubbed it between his fingers.

How to grab it without getting caught, killed, beaten up, or at the least stopped before we could destroy it, was the problem.

"He likes you," Losi said.

"And how do you figure that?"

"He's obsessed with you."

"Not the same."

"You have a past."

"Long passed."

"Hil."

So it was up to me.

Up to me to do what exactly, we weren't sure. Johns needed to trust me, we figured. I needed to find some opportunity where his guard was down, where I could grab the chip. On the compound, any opportunity like that would end in getting caught immediately. My best bet was to go offsite with him, on a Do Bad Trip, and try to snatch it and run when we were somewhere out in the open. There was an unlikely success rate there too.

"Maybe we just shouldn't bother," Losi said.

"We?"

"You."

"We can't do nothing."

"We?"

"I."

#

"Hey, Hil," Johns said offhandedly as he passed my cell. I normally didn't answer, so he just kept walking without waiting for a response.

"Hey!" I called back.

He slowed down, turned around, smiled, shook his head, and walked off.

#

The next day he stopped in front of my cell. Wrapped his hands around the bars, leaned his forehead against them.

"Hey," he tried it again.

"Hey," I said, simply, and looked back down at *Walden*, diligently following along the lines with my index finger.

"Watcha reading?" he asked.

"I only have one book," I shrugged.

He let out a laugh-like sound. "Oh yeah."

I wasn't sure what to say next. I felt nervous, like I was actually flirting with him. With his big dumb smile, his forehead pressing eagerly in, he looked like Johns–the old Johns I knew— a person and not an idea.

Things went on this way. Each day he stopped by and we said a few words to each other. My plan seemed to work, but there was something sad in it, seeing him smile at me, his relief that we were becoming friends again.

I was treated more respectfully when I was moved in and out of my cell. No one tripped me or spit at me. I was allowed to walk without anyone holding my arms. No one had slapped me since the first day I said "Hey."

#

"Hey," I said one day as he approached, getting there first with the magic words.

"Hil," he said, trying not to smile, nodding at me.

"Remember peppermint patties?" I asked.

He shook his head, laughed. "Of course. Why?"

I shrugged. "I don't know. I was just thinking about them for some reason. Probably because I am hungry and they sound good."

His smile faded a little. I shouldn't have reminded him that he was starving me.

"Anyway I was just remembering that time at Chele's house."

"When you locked yourself in the bathroom?"

I nodded.

#

Peppermint patties were one of those disgusting concoctions that only people not old enough to legally drink enjoyed. They were simple: a shot of peppermint schnapps, chased by a squirt of chocolate syrup. They tasted delicious. They made everyone throw up.

In high school, shortly after we discovered the delicacy, Chele threw a party while her parents were out of town.

"Let's drink?" the invite said.

Drink we did.

At some point, everyone decided I'd had enough peppermint patties. I was told to stop. I did not like those instructions. I grabbed a bottle of Schnapps and a bottle of chocolate syrup and I locked myself in the bathroom so I could have "just one more."

I had one more and then I threw up chocolate brown liquid in Chele's bathroom. The toilet wouldn't flush.

# #

Johns unlocked my cell, came in, sat down on the mat beside me.

"That seems so long ago," he said.

"It was," I reminded him.

"We're old."

I nodded.

It was quiet for a few seconds. I scratched a mosquito bite on my elbow. Johns looked down at the cement floor.

"It's nice talking to you like this again," he said.

I didn't say anything.

"I never thought when we broke up... I thought we'd still be friends."

"Johns," I had to think about what I would say carefully. "We aren't not friends because we broke up."

"I know."

"I mean a lot of other stuff has happened..."

"I know."

# #

"I dreamed about you last night," he told me the next day. "We were in my bedroom at my parents' house. Remember it?"

"You still had a race car bed when you were in high school."

"Exactly! I came in my room and you were sitting on my race car bed. You looked like you, adult you, and I looked like me, adult me, but we were dressed like we did when we were teenagers. You had your shoes off and your feet crossed and were wearing those pink socks with white peace signs on them."

"God I wish I still had those!"

"I came in the room and you said, 'Hi, Johns,' and I said 'What are you doing here?' And you said you were there to study, that we had a big test the next day. So you took out a textbook and opened it up but all that was on the pages were pictures of you and copies of the letters you used to send me.

"I asked you why we needed to study that and you said 'you don't think it's important?' I said well, sure it was important, but I didn't think it would be on the test. You were mad and you got off the race car bed and left."

I shrugged. "Dream interpretation?"

"Well, that one's not very hard to interpret."

"I guess not."

"When I saw you at Georgie's party, you were all glittery and joyful. It made me want to just scoop you up and take you with me."

"Is that why you wanted to convince me to join HDT?"

"I don't know. I'm sorry, Hil," he murmured.

I looked at him, trying to figure out if he meant it. He avoided eye contact, got up, and left.

"Hil?" he approached slowly, quietly.

"You can come in if you want," I said. I realized I actually wanted him to.

It was early morning. The air was cool and moist. If I closed my eyes and listened to the footsteps in the dirt, the birds chirping, I might think I was somewhere nice, might understand little Losi visiting, dipping her toe in the water.

"It's a pretty day," I said just to say something.

"Yeah. Listen, I need to talk to you about something."

He seemed nervous, kept pulling on a loose thread on the hem of his pants.

"I know we've been... friendly I guess lately, but I was wondering... Are you in now?"

"In?"

"In. In HDT. Are you in or are you out, that sort of thing..."

"Oh."

"Well?"

In was what I needed to be for this plan, but I had to be believably in, to have come around after being out for so long.

"I'm trying to be in."

TWENTY-TWO

Seoraksan Park contained Mt. Seoraksan and The Unification Buddha, or Tongil Daebul, a 48-foot tall, bronze, seated Buddha built in 1997 to symbolize the South Korean people's wish to be reunited with the North. The Buddha sat atop a lotus flower, the base of which housed a small shrine. After so many years, the Buddha seemed more of a sad reminder of reality than any beacon of hope. One day, the park closed. Large barriers were placed around its perimeter and work trucks moved in and out. The view of the mountain, and the Buddha, could not be blocked, but no one knew what was happening on the ground.

When the park reopened, it looked much the same: nice paths up the mountain, sky gondolas, food carts, and cafes, but the shrine inside the Buddha was closed to the public, and the sign out front read "VS Welcomes You."

# #

Ronnie, Gret, Colin, Lin, and RIFF23 arrived at VS Park as morning broke. There were a few visitors snapping pictures with the mountains behind them, sticking their heads through photo ops, eating roasted chestnuts.

The Buddha loomed large, the mountains larger. Ronnie felt his heart rate increase, his stomach clench. "Large structures make me nervous," he said to no one in particular.

They didn't know what they were doing, which didn't help. Lin communicated with his friend in HDT as best he could, which meant whenever she was able to sneak off with her Screen. She knew when the attack would happen and that Hil would be there.

As they approached the Buddha, they noticed a small group congregated beside a row of candles.

"Slow down," Ronnie hissed. "That's them." He saw Hil bending down to light a candle, Johns's hand on her back. Two guys with their arms crossed stood behind them, looking back and forth diligently.

Lin motioned for everyone to duck behind the wall that bordered the Buddha. There was no new movement at the temple, no sign that they'd been spotted.

"Let's go for it I guess," Lin said.

"Such encouragement," Gret said.

"Well, it's not much but it's what we got."

With that, RIFF23 engaged his strobe light function and started screeching "Alert! Alert! Alert!" and rolling quickly toward the group by the candles. They looked toward him, frozen for a second, then radiated out in jagged backward steps.

Ronnie, Colin and Gret ran toward the group. Lin circled around behind the wall, toward the back of the temple. Ronnie ran straight for Johns. Hil had staggered a few steps away from him, was widening her eyes in recognition at RIFF23 and Ronnie, confusion at the other two figures running furiously toward her. RIFF23 stopped when he reached the candles, turned, and started making wide circles through the scattered group, continuing his alert message and strobe light.

Johns looked around for Hil, made his way toward her, then saw Ronnie. "What the..." he started.

Ronnie punched him in the face.

Ronnie had never punched anyone in the face before. It was awkward and limp and he made a terrible sound. He thought his hand might be broken. He cradled it, looked at Johns, who didn't look like someone who had been punched in the face. His nose was not bleeding, his head was not bent. Ronnie ran at him and headbutted him in the chest.

Johns let out a little chuckle. "Whoa there, buddy. You alright?"

Ronnie kicked him in the knee.

Johns was less amused. He grabbed Ronnie, pulled his arms behind his back, held him there. "Hil!" he called. Hil stood a few feet away, looking back and forth. "Hil, come here!" Johns said.

She walked over. The other two HDTers were running away from RIFF23. Gret and Colin were nowhere in sight.

"Hil, you see who this is?" Johns asked.

Hil nodded.

"You know he was going to be here?"

She shook her head.

"What do you think?" He whispered in Ronnie's ear. "Should I trust her?"

Ronnie said nothing. He looked out to see Lin walking around the outer wall. RIFF23, Colin, Gret, and the other HDTers were gone.

"We don't have time for this. Teddy!" Johns called. One of the HDTers appeared from around the side of the Buddha, pointing a gun. Johns shoved Ronnie toward him. Teddy grabbed Ronnie's arm and pulled him off.

"Johns, I didn't know. I swear!" Ronnie heard Hil say as Teddy forced him away.

As they rounded the corner, Ronnie caught sight of RIFF23, Colin, and Gret, shoved against the side of the Buddha, the other guard swinging his gun at even intervals between each of them.

"I'm all backed up," RIFF23 said. "You don't need to bother pointing it at me."

Teddy shoved Ronnie beside Colin.

"Guns," Colin muttered to him. "I knew we forgot something."

"Shut up!" both guards yelled.

Ronnie considered the fact that he failed. He found Hil, but he did not save her. He wondered if he would be killed, or thrown into North Korea, or forced to join HDT.

Colin elbowed Ronnie in the side. Ronnie grunted, "What the hell, man?" Colin shushed him, barely nodded out toward the guards. Ronnie followed Colin's eyes. The wall that circled around the Buddha was a few feet behind the guards. Lin stood behind it, his torso and head visible. He waved at them and made the motion of plugging his ears. They stared at him blankly. He pointed at them and did the motion again.

"Cover your ears," Gret whispered, keeping her teeth gritted.

They did.

"What the hell are you doing?" one of the guards asked.

Just then, RIFF23 emitted an unbearably loud, high-pitched screech. Even with his ears covered, Ronnie felt it deep into his brain. He fell to his knees. So did Colin and Gret. So did the guards. Lin ran up behind the guards, grabbed one of their guns, and hit them each hard in the back of the head. They collapsed.

RIFF23 stopped the screeching. The others uncovered their ears, and stood up, wincing.

"That was awesome!" Lin yelled.

RIFF23 played a champagne-popping emoji.

The others rubbed their ears.

"Sorry!" Lin yelled, and pulled out his earplugs.

"What are you doing out here?" Ronnie asked. "Why aren't you in there?"

# #

"After we create the distraction, I'll run in ahead of them. I'll wait in the server room. Hopefully it'll be Johns and Hil there, and I'll jump out. Hil will help me."

That was the plan—as much of it as could be planned— they'd gone over the night before. The plan was not for Lin to come back out of the temple and signal RIFF23 to use sonic weaponry.

# #

"I couldn't get in," Lin said.

There was a retina scanner in the entrance to VS, in the closet of the temple. That was how Lin went to work each day, standing there with his eye wide until a polite, feminine voice said, "Thank you and work hard," and the door swung open. This time, the feminine voice, still friendly as ever, said, "Access denied." Lin punched restart, tried again. "Access denied," the voice said. "You are not authorized to enter this building. Thank you and work hard."

"How's Hil going to get in past the retina thing?" Ronnie asked.

Lin shook his head. "I don't know."

"How's she going to stop Johns by herself?"

"I don't know. I got to her, though. When you were fighting Johns. I told her there's a gun I stashed in the server room. That's all I can do for her now."

"A gun? She doesn't know how to shoot a gun!"

Lin rubbed a hand through his hair, heaved a sigh.

"We need to get away from these guys," he motioned toward the two guards.

They walked around to the other side of the Buddha and crouched behind the wall outside the temple entrance.

"It seems like you might have had that sound idea in your back pocket," Gret said, pulling on her earlobes.

"Yeah," Lin shrugged.

"So maybe you could have given us all earplugs?"

"Huh. Yeah. Guess so."

TWENTY-THREE

Losi was a figurehead. She was the founder. She was allowed her privacy: her own cabin down by the lake, strolls through the woods that were monitored from a distance, meals taken at home, not in the mess hall.

She was not the leader anymore, no one thought she was, but they were there because of her, and that garnered some respect. There were certain expectations of her, the quiet woman with a shaved head who valued seclusion. She must be wise, she must see the unseen, she must be above the things of this world. It was a part for her to play, something to pass the time, and she slipped into it easily, comfortably, unsure if it was still a role or if it was just her.

She read tea leaves and tarot cards and palms. She asked people: "When were you born?" and then nodded knowingly: "An Aries!"

Some came to her for a consultation. They could never be about anything concrete, about the commune or the activities of HDT, only about the stars, the universe, personalities, and love. Within these questions about higher matters, she sensed an unease, a desire to ask, instead of "Will I ever find love?"—"Am I in the right place?" or "Are we doing wrong?"

She was kind. She told everyone they would find love, that it would be a lucky month, that she saw strength in their future. There were tea leaves scattered at the bottom of a cup, bleak faces stared up at her from the tarot reading, lines on a hand. There was a pond beside her, woods behind her, a hopeful face in front of her, a terrorist organization surrounding her.

Finn wandered over to her cabin early one morning. Losi was sitting on her back stoop, sipping coffee, watching the darkness recede from the grass.

Losi jumped when she heard footsteps. "Who is it?" she called.

"Losi?"

She didn't recognize the voice.

The woman rounded the corner. She had sleek black hair pulled back in a tight ponytail. She looked at Losi shyly, eagerly, smiled a quick smile. If it weren't for the faint lines around her eyes when she grew closer, or the tone of her voice, Losi might have thought she was a child. She was not particularly small or undeveloped, just timid and innocent-seeming.

"I'm Finn," she said.

Losi nodded. "I've seen you around."

"I was wondering if I could have some tea?" she asked. She kept her hands in her back pockets and stared at the ground.

"I don't know if I'm mentally ready for a reading yet," Losi said. That's what she said when she didn't feel like doing one.

"Oh. No. Not a reading. Just some tea?"

"I'm having coffee. Would you like some of that?"

Finn shrugged, said: "Sure."

Losi poured her a cup and Finn joined her on the steps. A chipmunk ran up. Stopped for a moment at their feet, sniffed, and continued into the woods.

"I saw your video," Finn said.

Losi didn't say anything.

"That's sort of why I came here." She blew on the coffee. "But when I got here, I saw you around, but, it seems like... you're not in charge."

"No."

"Well, I... I noticed you look, sort of... Are you OK?"

Losi gave her a tight smile. "Sure. I'm OK."

"OK. Well. Good." She sipped the coffee, shook her head. "I really hate coffee, sorry." She set it down on the step between them. "Can I tell you something honest?"

"Sure."

"I'm not OK here."

# #

Johns seemed more cheerful than usual.

"Hil, if you are in, then I've got a job for you."

I gave him a thumbs up, decided that was stupid, and smiled stupidly, sticking my hand behind my back. He stayed outside, face striped by the bars.

"You and me. We're going overseas."

"Vacation?"

"Sort of."

I waited.

"Hil, do you know what our followers want us to do?"

I held my hands out, palms up, as if to say: "How could I?"

"They want us to attack VS."

"That seems like a big job."

Johns grinned. "It is. It really is. But you know what? I'm going to make it even bigger!"

"How's that?"

"We're not going to bomb them."

I realized I'd been holding my breath. I released the air, my shoulders loosened.

"We're going to hack them."

I froze. "Hack?"

"Yep."

"Why?"

"So we can release all of their information."

"The companies'?"

"The clients'."

"That's what your followers want?"

"Sure. Right? Makes sense. VS controls the minds of our people. Controls their bank accounts. Controls their lives. Let's put it all out there. Let's show people for who they really are. Let's show VS for what they really are. Everyone will be shocked when they see how much of their personal data is stored."

"It's stored, yes, but it's still technically private."

"Until VS decides to make it public."

"But you're deciding to make it public."

"Exactly! It's going to be like nothing they've ever seen before."

# #

"We have contact!" Losi whispered to me that night. Most of the commune was at the mess hall, a few walked by us, nodding politely.

"The stars have aligned!" she said.

"You been doing a lot of palm readings today?"

"A girl came to me today. She has a Screen."

"Shut up."

"It's true."

"And she's not tricking you?"

"How should I know? But she has a Screen. She wants out. She says we can use it."

"VS," I told her.

"VS?"

"The next target. A leak of their data. See what she can do with that."

"A leak? To who?"

"To everyone I guess."

"Why?"

"He gave me reasons. They don't make sense."

"I've been thinking about that. About things that don't make sense. Like the chip."

"Yeah?"

"What kind of threat is that?"

"A pretty bad one."

"Sure, but, why would he do it?"

"Do what?"

"Leak it. Sell it. Whatever it is he thinks he's going to do with it. That goes against this place... whatever's become of it... That goes against what Johns is supposed to believe."

"Maybe he doesn't believe anything."

"I don't know."

"Can she try to get to my parents? On the Screen?"

Before I boarded the plane, I was given a bath. They took me into a tent, built like my ZT. Effie boiled the water and filled up a big wooden tub. She sat loyally by me and scrubbed my bony back, massaged my greasy scalp. Dawn had not yet broken and the tent was lit with candles. The darkness amplified the contrasting shades of life: deepened the circles under her eyes, strange bruises on her arms. I lay back with my eyes closed, remembering something about my old life, something of comfort and safety.

"I wonder what you really think about all this," I said to her, quietly, keeping my eyes closed.

I heard the sound of her ringing out the rag, laying it on the side of the tub, sitting back on her heels.

"All this is what's happening," she said.

TWENTY-FOUR

There was a gun in the server room.

Teddy pulled Ronnie away. Johns shoved me in the opposite direction.

Lin hid a gun in the server room.

We rounded the Buddha. Buddha had his eyes closed. He looked pleased.

The safety is on, Lin told me.

The doors to the temple were open. There were no worshippers inside, a few candles at the end of their wicks flickered. We went into a closet filled with brown robes. Johns parted the robes and opened a door.

It's under the terminal to the right when you first walk in, Lin said.

"Lean forward," Johns said. He pushed my face toward a round console on the wall. A light scanned my eye.

"Thank you and work hard," a pleasant voice said, and a door opened in front of me.

"Go. Wait for me on the other side," Johns said.

The door closed. I was alone in a long hallway. The walls were decorated with framed photographs of beautiful women, posing in casual clothes, with light make-up, the same satisfied look on their faces as the Buddha. Down the center of the hall ran two moving sidewalks.

The door behind me opened, and Johns came through. "Alright," he said gruffly. "Let's go." He stepped onto the sidewalk moving away from us and started walking quickly.

I ran after him. "Johns, what is going on?"

"I was going to ask you that." He looked at me coldly.

"What do you mean?"

"You expect me to believe your ex-boyfriend is here and you didn't know anything about it?"

"How could I?"

He clenched his hands at his side. He hadn't slapped me since I turned nice and seemed to be rethinking it.

"Let's just get on with it."

"What is this place?"

"What do you mean?"

"This is VS?"

"Part of it."

"Where is everyone?"

"Do you think I'm some kind of idiot? Do you think I would plan an attack at a time when people were around?"

"It's day time, middle of the week. They work only at night?"

"Something like that."

"They don't have 24 hour security? Cameras? Alarms?"

"I've taken care of it. I know what I'm doing." He sounded defensive.

The sidewalk ended and we came to a bank of elevators. He pushed my eye toward another round console. The elevator door opened and the voice said "Going up!" The doors closed behind me and I waited for him. When he got on I said:

"And how is that thing scanning my eye?"

"You ask too many questions."

My dad collected VHS players, camcorders, old writable tapes picked up at garage sales with bits of television shows recorded on them. When I was young, I used to do little routines for my parents: one-act plays, interpretive dance, recitations of poems–all very bad results of no formal teaching in the arts. I was fascinated by myself. We would stick the tapes in, gather around the rounded TV, and watch the grainy footage. "There you are," my mom would say, and I would stare in wonder.

There I was. Those were my hands, a little big for my frame, clasped in front of me, that was my hair, frizzy, unruly, cowlicked, those were my chapped lips and skinny legs, and that was my voice, strange and high, just shy of a lisp.

I liked to rewind: watch myself walk backwards, out of the room, see myself disappear, then hit play, see myself again. "There I am," I'd say.

Years later, when I couldn't sleep, I'd rewind that day with Johns. I'd watch myself—hands still big, hair still frizzy, legs skinnier from my stint in captivity—walk backwards, out of the server room, down the hall, down the elevator, onto the moving sidewalk, and back out into the temple. From there, the rewind splintered. I couldn't hit play and watch it all happen the same way, like I did with my childhood videos, I had to splice something new onto the tape. Sometimes I took a handful of those brown robes, threw them at John, ran for it. Ronnie waited outside the door and we disappeared into the woods. When I felt angriest, I rewound all the way to when Teddy appeared with the gun to drag Ronnie off. I grabbed the gun, shot Teddy, shot Johns. Sometimes I pulled the candles off the altar and set the Buddha on fire.

None of these scenarios were particularly realistic, but I could have done something, anything.

# #

We went up to the 13th floor. There was no one in the hallways, no muffled voices behind doors, no footsteps. All the lights were on. Johns led me to the end of the hall. Our eyes were scanned again and we entered a cold, giant room filled with banks and banks of computers. The room was long and narrow. From the entrance, I could not see where it ended.

I shivered by the door, oriented myself, looked for the terminal to the right when I first walked in. Where Lin said he hid the gun. Johns walked farther into the room.

"Come on!" he said.

I reached down like I was going to tie my shoe, looked under the terminal. It was there, taped to the bottom. A pistol, I thought. I didn't know anything about guns, but it was a small gun. A handgun, I guessed. It could fit in a hand. I grabbed it, shoved it in my back pocket, ran to catch up with Johns.

"I don't think I'm going to be much help to you here," I said. I wasn't sure why I felt like chatting. "I don't know anything about computers, you know."

"Don't worry, Hil. You'll do fine," he said. His voice was oddly comforting. For a moment, I forgot I didn't actually need to be reassured by him that I would be successful at hacking a multinational corporation.

We walked with no clear destination. Johns kept a steady pace and didn't look around. I assumed he knew where he was going.

Finally we reached a giant Screen at the end of the room. It showed a smiling emoji, like the one RIFF23 used when he was in a good mood.

"Hello," it said as we approached.

"Please scan now."

We stood there. Johns looked at me.

"Hello," the Screen said again.

"Please scan now."

The safety is on.

I had heard of safeties in movies. Knew it was something on the gun I needed to push or flip to get it to shoot. I hoped I would be able to figure out what it was when I pulled it out.

"Hello."

"Please scan now."

Johns just stood there, looking at the Screen.

I pulled out the gun. I tried to sound sure of myself, to gulp down my shaking voice. "We're not doing this."

Johns wasn't facing me, but could see my reflection in the smiley-face-emblazoned Screen. He held his hands up, turned slowly toward me.

"OK, Hil," he said. His face looked scared. His voice was shaking too, I noticed. "I'll do whatever you want," he said.

This threw me for a second. Johns had known me most of my life. Did he think I knew how to shoot a gun? That I would shoot a gun? I had not expected this to work.

"OK," I said, still trying to sound like I knew what I was doing. "OK. Good."

With that, his hands still in the air, he turned back toward the Screen. "This isn't right, Hil. This is private information."

I didn't say anything. Was he agreeing with me? Was the gun all I needed to get him to come to his senses?

Then he slowly leaned forward, toward the round console.

"What are you..." I started.

"You're making a big mistake," he said.

"Scan complete. Access granted," the Screen said.

A key pad popped out and he started typing. "This will ruin lives," he said.

I noticed that the arm holding the gun had lowered so that it was pointing at the floor. I picked it up, walked closer to him. Pushed the gun against his head.

"What the fuck are you doing?" I asked.

"I'm doing what you asked, Hil," he said. "I'm going as fast as I can."

I dropped the gun. I ran out of the server room, down the hall, down the elevator, onto the moving sidewalk, and back out into the temple.

TWENTY-FIVE

Maybe it was because everything else was climactic that having her back with him felt so anticlimactic. There she was beside him and he felt no heart-in-the-throat joy, no special desire to get up in the morning. What he felt was normal.

This despite the abnormality of being holed up in South Korea in hiding, unsure from what.

#

Shortly after they left the Buddha—the Buddha that Ronnie was sure he felt a heebie jeebiness about not purely because of its largeness, but because of an inherent evil lurking therein—the alerts started.

"Breaking news," RIFF23 informed them.

At this point they were in a CAR with Lin, not sure where he was taking them, because they hadn't bothered to ask.

"We're a little busy for news now, bud," Ronnie pointed out.

"Breaking news," a woman's voice came from RIFF23's Screen.

"I just said..." Ronnie started.

RIFF23 paused the feed for a moment. "Trust me," he said, then continued to play the video.

"We have just received word of a major attack on VS headquarters, located in VS Park, South Korea. Just minutes ago, all of the company's customer records were publicly released. A VS spokesperson informs us that the headquarters were vacant during the time of the attack, due to planned maintenance. Shocking video and audio pulled from the VS security system shows an unknown woman pointing a gun at the head of Johns Calum, son of NSA Director Ford Calum, and forcing him to scan his retina in order to access VS data. VS confirms that Johns is an employee with full security clearance."

The footage cut to Hil pointing a gun at Johns and Johns saying "OK, Hil. I'll do whatever you want," and leaning his face toward the retina scanner.

"That's not what happened," Hil said.

No one said anything.

"They cut out all the other stuff... How did they...Where's all the other stuff?"

#

Lin took them to his grandfather's house. He lived by the ocean, on a steep hill, in a brick block house with large windows and a skinny porch, situated on the bend in a narrow road, across the street from a stained convenience store.

The grandfather nodded and smiled at them as they entered. He sat on the floor watching his Screen. He said something to Lin, then pointed at the Screen.

Korean reporters were talking over the same video footage of Hil pointing the gun at Johns's head.

"Shit," Lin said. "Come on."

They went upstairs to an open loft, with mats stacked in a corner. RIFF23 pulled up another news story.

"Joining us now from South Korea and Washington D.C. respectively, are Johns and Ford Calum."

"Thanks for having us," Johns stood in front of the Unification Buddha. His eyes darted around like he was afraid of something and he kept his arms close to his body.

"Johns, can you tell us what happened?"

"Well... Hil... She... she wanted to go on a trip."

"And who is Hil, Johns?"

"Hil. She's... she was... my girlfriend. And she told me she wanted to go on a trip to South Korea. I said 'sure,' since my work has an office here and everything."

"This was Hil Mills, correct?"

"Yes."

"The daughter of Bill and Laura Mills?"

"Yes."

"For those just joining us, Johns Calum confirms that he was forced at gunpoint by his girlfriend Hil Mills to access confidential VS client information, which she then leaked. Hil Mills is daughter of Bill and Laura Mills, Tech billionaires and famous off the gridders... So, Johns, you took Hil to VS Park?"

"No. Well, yes. That wasn't the plan, though. I told her they were closed for maintenance. She said wouldn't it be funny if we just tried to go in... If I used my access privileges. It was stupid of me to agree. She's been acting strange lately. She went away for a while a few weeks back. She got really into that HDT group. She's really radical about all of that sort of stuff. So we went in and she asked me to show her around. She said she wanted to see the servers. I took her in there. And... and..." he started stammering, tearing up.

"It's OK, Johns. Whenever you're ready."

"And then she pulled a gun out, told me to scan my retina. I didn't know what to do!"

"Joining us now is Johns's father, Ford Calum, Director of the NSA. Thank you for being with us Mr. Calum."

Ford sat behind a wide, mahogany desk, framed photos of his family prominent in the foreground, an American flag pin on his lapel.

"Thank you for having me," he said sternly.

"Mr. Calum can you tell us about this Hil Mills individual, and about the group HDT with which she is associated?"

"Hil Mills is a violent, dangerous person. She was raised in an off the grid family and radicalized. We don't know if she was radicalized by the group HDT or before, but the group itself is known for dangerous, terrorist attacks, all in the name of so-called privacy and freedom from technology. What kind of freedom and privacy they are getting by leaking the information of millions of innocent people, I don't know. Let's not forget that she's the rumored inventor of the Zen Tent, a current danger to so many of our young people!"

There was a raid on HDT. They watched as members filed down the dirt road, handcuffed, pushed into waiting police CARS. Hil spotted Effie, smiling and sticking her tongue out at the cameras.

Then there was Losi. "Cult Leader: Losi West," flashed on the screen as she walked with police officers on either side. She looked up at the camera, her face neither defeated nor triumphant. She looked away, toward the woods.

Lin knew a guy. The guy changed out RIFF23's serial number, explained how they should dismantle their Screens and scatter the parts. They dug holes in ditches along the road at night.

Lin found them an apartment behind a barbershop. The couple that owned it smiled and nodded as he spoke quietly to them, gestured toward the foreigners. Ronnie and Hil stayed in one room, Gret and Colin in another, a tiny bathroom in between. Hil's face was everywhere, but the owners seemed disinterested in this fact, only exchanging friendly hellos and goodbyes.

At night, Ronnie and Hil walked down to the beach and watched the squid boats glow on the water, listened to the rhythm of the waves against the concrete pilings.

"It's strange," Hil said. "I'm kind of happy here."

Ronnie squeezed her hand and made a mental note to ask Lin why the bottom of the boats glowed. He could not look it up.

On clear mornings, Gret and Colin got up early, walked down the beach. By lunch they returned, salt-scented, carrying sea glass.

Ronnie and Hil speculated about what went on in their room, but whenever they happened to peek in the door there were two mats laid out several feet apart, and neat piles of clothing in two separate corners. Sometimes when it was quiet, Ronnie heard them murmuring, laughing, falling into silence.

Letters came.

Ronnie watched Hil as she read what Losi wrote. Her face grew still and tight, a line cutting through her forehead. She began shaking her head back and forth. She did not sob or shake, just cried silently, wiped her eyes, blew her nose, folded the letter back up into its standard-issue envelope.

And one day familiar voices in the barbershop.

"This is her!" a loud, male voice boomed. "Right here. Daughter!"

Hil and Ronnie were napping, hot, each with one leg out from under the cover. Hil snorted, stirred, sat up. Ronnie rolled over and pulled the blanket over his head.

Some nights they stayed inside, waiting, unsure what they were waiting for.

EPILOGUE

My tea visions had promising beginnings–a future me visiting, telling me to follow her—but they all ended the same: in a field of dead grass, watching a red sunset.

On the last night of my final visit to Doper's Memory, Isis, Leonard, and I shared one last pot of trippy tea. When my vision came, it was Me of the Future, again.

"Follow me," she said.

"If you say so," I answered, "but you're starting to really let me down."

"I know, I know," she said, "But trust me this time."

"You say that every time!" I pointed out.

"Yes, but, well, you're going to follow me either way."

"I guess," I sighed and slowly followed her through Isis's back door.

She took me the typical way, weaving through the streets of DM, through the iron gate, into the field of dead grass.

"It's weird you call it the field of dead grass," Isis said once. "Usually, the field is lush and green. You just come here at a bad time."

This time, instead of sitting and staring at the trees and saying nothing like she normally did, future me sat in an A-frame tent. As I approached, I could see her shadow, sitting patiently, some light inside making the tent bright against the darkening sky. I pulled back the tent flap and saw her sitting on a pillow with a small candle in front of her.

There was another pillow across from her.

"Sit," she said. I found her voice annoyingly calm.

"Fine," I said. I sat. I stared at her, waiting. "Well?" I said, finally, after what would have been a period of uncomfortable silence if it were possible to feel uncomfortable around yourself.

"You're OK, Hil."

"Great! Thanks! Another expansion of the consciousness as usual."

She sighed. Future me was ever the martyr.

"Do you know where the word 'OK,' comes from, Hil?"

"No, Hil. No one does."

"I do."

"Of course you do."

"It's Choctaw."

"OF COURSE IT IS!"

"Calm down, Hil."

"You are the least original vision of all time. You're going to tell me about ancient Native American words?"

"Not ancient, Hil. Relatively recent if you think about how long the world has been in existence."

"I don't think about that, so..."

"You are hostile."

"I'm you. You should know."

"As I was saying, some believe that OK originated from the Choctaw word 'okeh' which meant 'it is so.'"

"That doesn't sound true."

She just smiled at me.

"So... You said 'You are OK,' So you wanted to tell me that I am it is so?"

"Yes."

"Can I leave?"

"Look around you, Hil."

I did. The tent was bare except for the two pillows, the candle, and our bodies. I peeked outside of the tent flap, but it was pitch black. "How do you feel in here?"

I sighed. "I guess it feels pretty nice."

"Safe?"

"Yeah, I guess that's a good word for it."

"OK."

"OK. I am trying to go along with this. So. Tell me," I gritted my teeth, "how 'it is so' relates to my life."

"It doesn't relate to your life, it is your life. You can't manage life. You can't plan it or change it or fix it. It just is. It is so."

"So. What? Give up?"

"No. Just go with it. Find what makes you feel safe and calm. Find it and stay there. Venture out sometimes so you don't fail to see what else is so, to see new things that make you feel safe and calm, or happy or even sad or scared. It is all so."

I actually felt a little better after this. "I actually feel a little better," I said.

"I know."

"How?"

"I'm you."

"So... you remember when you visited you?"

"Not exactly. I just know that hearing the things I said would make me feel better."

"Trippy."

"Exactly!"

Future Hil and I left the tent. She carried the candle and we ventured into the woods, dark and full of strange sounds. She asked me if I was scared and I said I was. She held my hand. I thought it would feel like nothing, holding my own hand, but it felt nice. It felt like I would be OK.

Acknowledgments

Thank you to Nate Ragolia and Shaunn Grulkowski for seeing something in this book and giving it a home. Thanks to Nate for the encouragement, advice, and for being such an enthusiastic, kind person with whom to take this journey.

Jonathan, I couldn't have done any of it without you. Thank you for reading, re-reading, discussing this book endlessly, and being my number one fan and helper. Thanks for walking the dogs and feeding me.

Thanks to Mom and Dad for the books and love and Michael, Anthony, and Joshua for the jokes.

About the Author

Sarah Colombo lives in Baton Rouge, Louisiana. This is her first book.

About the Publishing Team

Nate Ragolia was labeled as "weird" early in elementary school, and it stuck. He's a lifelong lover of science fiction, and a nerd/geek. In 2015 his first book, *There You Feel Free,* was published by 1888's Black Hill Press. He's also the author of *The Retroactivist*, published by Spaceboy Books. He founded and edits BONED, an online literary magazine, has created webcomics, and writes whenever he's not playing video games or petting dogs.

Rex Roberts (w/ an assist from visual artist Robert Brgoch) is a Denver-based designer, web consultant, and nonprofit biking and youth baseball advocate. He's a sci-fi fan, a sports aficionado, and an accomplished wearer of many hats.

Shaunn Grulkowski has been compared to Warren Ellis and Phillip K. Dick and was once described as what a baby conceived by Kurt Vonnegut and Margaret Atwood would turn out to be. He's at least the fifth best Slavic-Latino-American sci-fi writer in the Baltimore metro area. He's the author of *Retcontinuum,* and the editor of *A Stalled Ox* and *The Goldfish,* all for 1888/Black Hill Press.